Scar

Books by R. J. F.

<u>Tales of the Multiverse</u>
Book 1: Monster versus Mortal
Book 2: Sarah
Book 3: Scar
Book 4: Planet of Shadows
Book 5: The Mysterious Four

<u>Darphopia</u>
Darphopia: The Godless Land
Darphopia: The Godless Land Collector's Edition
Darphopia: The Second God War
Darphopia: The Second God War Collector's Edition

<u>R. J. F. Shorts</u>
The Seducter (e-book only)
The Council of Cats (e-book only)

<u>Gamebooks</u>
Pencilventure: The Ancient Forest Temple

Scar

R. J. F.

Cover and interior illustrations by R. J. F.
Beta read by Nicole "Nikki" Fyffe

Dedicated to my cousin Connor, the creator of the
character "B. B.", and the person who used to write
endless stories with me in our youth.

My story began much like that of any other fourteen-year-old boy: sitting in the basement eating the kinds of snacks that would make a dentist cry and playing the kinds of videogames that every adult I know swears will kill off all my brain cells eventually. To paint a picture of me, I was small, dark-skinned, and had brown eyes and short hair. I was also surprisingly skinny for the amount of chips I ate, but I digress.

The basement was tiny but cozy and only lit by the light of the flashing television screen—the size of the room was because my family's not rich, but the light source being the television screen, that was a choice. The clacking of the buttons on my controller was echoing off the white walls, and that echo ricocheted off ... well, nothing, really. The basement was actually kind of empty, now I think about it.

Anyway, that's the scene set. Now here's where my average life took a turn.

"Alex, can you come upstairs for a minute?" my mother called.

"Does it have to be now? I'm a little busy," I said, not daring to let my annoyance show through my voice, but trust me, I was pretty annoyed.

"Busy, huh? With what? A game?"

"Well, when you put it that way, it doesn't sound like a valid reason, but it totally is," I explained. "Trust me."

"Alex, the last time I trusted you, I bought a five-hundred-dollar game console." She likes to use that one against me a lot, a reference to the not-being-rich thing.

"Money well spent if you ask me."

"You know, last time I checked, videogames had a pause button."

"Would you believe this one doesn't?"

"Alex." Oof, the tone. The perfect way to tell a kid they're pushing their luck.

"Fine, I'm coming." I paused the game and headed upstairs.

I emerged from the basement—a bit like a mole who isn't used to the bright sunlight—and squinted around at the wooden floors and red walls of the hallway until locking my gaze on my mother.

She met me at the top of the stairs and stared down at me. We're pretty much identical—you know, aside from the fact that she's a girl, and her hair is a big ball of cotton that came straight out of the 70s. Plus, she was, like, forty years old.

"Oh, Alex." She sighed and then hugged me.

"Uh, I know you love me, Mom, but if this is the only reason I had to come upstairs, I literally had better things to do."

"What could be better than a hug from your mom?"

"Everything. Literally everything."

She chuckled. "You always know how to make me laugh, Alex."

"I don't remember giving a punch line," I muttered.

There was a sadness in her voice. She placed her hand on my cheek, and it was sweaty and cold; something must have been bothering her. "Mom, are you okay?"

"Fine, honey, just fine." Her lie was so clearly exposed by her tone. "It's just ... well, I have to go away for a while."

"Go away? Where?"

"I'm ... not sure."

"Well, how long will you be gone?"

"I don't know, honey."

"Does Dad know you're leaving?"

"I left him a voicemail."

"But you can't just ..." I was silent, trying to keep my thoughts straight.

She exhaled. "Alex, I need you to promise me something."

"What?"

There were tears in her eyes, but she held them back. "I need you to promise me that you'll be a good boy and

..." She bit her lip nervously, but she never looked away from me. "Alex, remember that you always have a choice."

"What are you talking about? What choice?"

She looked away quickly, as if she heard someone calling, but I didn't hear anything. "I'm sorry, Alex, I have to go." She kissed my forehead. "Be good."

Then she took off, heading for the front door. I stood there at the top of the stairs for a second, struggling to have a coherent thought. I couldn't think. What would you do if your mom said that to you? Where was she going? How long would she be gone? ... Why did it feel like she wouldn't be coming back?

If I was going to get answers to any of those questions, I had to act fast. I followed her down the hallway, through the living room and out the front door. She was walking briskly down the suburban street, shrouded in the darkness of night. I kept close behind, mirroring her speed but keeping my distance as well. I didn't think she would want me following her. Maybe she was going somewhere dangerous.

After five minutes or so, we arrived at an open field near my house, separating the suburban streets from the busy highway. It was here that my eyes locked onto something I'd never seen before, some kind of humanoid creatures, two of them. Both were dressed in white and floated atop the grassy ground. They were slender, pale, and had dents in their faces where their eyes and mouths should have been.

The creatures seemed to welcome my mom—not with words but with inviting hand gestures. She accepted the invitation and walked between them, and as I blinked my eyes, she was gone.

At this point, caution was out the window. Cursing myself for blinking, I ran after my mom, hoping that I would end up wherever she went by walking between the creatures as well. But I was unsuccessful. One of the creatures raised its hand, and I was gently levitated off the ground and placed about three metres away. Both creatures shook their heads disapprovingly, then I blinked, and they were gone, too.

I stood silently for a moment, my tiny, teenage brain struggling to process what had happened. Then I concluded that this must have been a bad dream. The weird way my mom was talking to me, the alien creatures that just sort of abducted her—yep, definitely a dream. Maybe if I just pinched myself hard enough, I'd wake up, and things would begin to make sense again. I tried a few times, but nothing changed except the number of bruises on my hand. I wasn't yet convinced that this was real, though. It was time for plan B: Go home, go to bed, and wake up the next morning. If you fall asleep in a dream, you wake up in real life. I'm sure that's a rule written down somewhere.

I started back home, pretending that this was a perfectly normal, not-weird-at-all evening. When I arrived, though, things just got weirder.

My dad had just got in from work. He parked the car on the drive, got out, and started walking away from the house. He didn't even close the car door. I stared at him; he looked different. His eyes were glowing red, and he wasn't particularly muscular or anything, but I swear I could see his veins bulging ... and they were pitch black.

He walked as if in a trance. I waved at him, even called his name, and although he stopped and stared right at me, he was unresponsive.

He turned and started to walk again, and I followed cautiously. After maybe ten minutes or so, we made it to the local shopping plaza, and I saw him duck behind a large store building, near some stacked-up wooden crates. I crept behind the store, too, and if everything else that had happened tonight weren't cause for a panic attack, then this certainly was. My dad stood next to a six-foot-tall, shadowy creature with sharp teeth, squinted red eyes, and a single nostril. It had what looked like a heart that was half submerged into its chest, pumping a rich, black ooze through its exposed veins. It was the same black colour as my dad's veins.

The sight of it alone kicked me into fight or flight. I dashed out of view, behind the nearby crates, and peeked timidly at the scene.

A second creature—identical to the first—emerged from a shadow on the wall—as in, literally came out of the shadow. The first creature kneeled before the second.

"Rise," said the second creature, with a deep and demonic voice.

The first creature stood.

"You may speak," said the second creature.

"Thank you, sir," said the first.

"How have the tests been going?"

"They have been proceeding well. We'll have to thank the Faction Leader in Dimension-002. Their extraction of the hybrid's DNA will prove useful in combating the threat of the interdimensional traveller."

"I'm afraid the Faction Leader of Dimension-002 is dead."

The first creature was silent. Shock maybe?

"The girl, Sarah Pickaro, killed them," the second creature explained.

"I see."

"And I understand that the interdimensional traveller has collected her as well."

"Now there are five." The first one gritted its teeth.

"Indeed. We need to combat this swiftly, so I hope you have something useful for me."

The first creature glanced at my dad before continuing; my dad didn't have any reaction to these things. "With your permission, sir, I would like to use the hybrid's data to create an army of hybrid creatures who will fight in our stead, allowing us to focus on rebuilding the population."

"According to the Faction Leader in Dimension-002, the girl was extremely hostile," said the second creature.

"She is powerful, perhaps more powerful even than are we, and she is unpredictable. How can you be certain this army will comply?"

The first creature grinned. "I have created a formula using the hybrid's data with some minor alterations. With it, I have created a serum that I've already injected into one of this dimension's locals." The creature presented my dad to the second creature, roughly pulling him in. "This first subject showed remarkable results. It possesses all the abilities the hybrid possesses, and its allegiance is to us and us alone.

"The serum had to be injected at birth, as I have discovered that the results are more favourable when the formula is introduced at a young age. I have also elected to separate the subject's experiences as a hybrid from the rest of its brain, giving me the ability to turn the subject on and off at a mental command. Allow me to demonstrate."

My dad's eyes reverted to their original, brown colour. He stared around nervously. "What the hell! Where am I?" he spluttered. Before he could say or do anything else, though, his eyes turned red again, and he was silent.

"Impressive." The second creature grinned.

"I'm pleased to hear you say that," replied the first.

"You are permitted to proceed with Project Hybrid, and I hope to see results in a timely manner. I expect the years we've spent here hidden from the abeedoids and the interdimensional traveller will not last indefinitely. Cease communication."

The first creature responded, not with words, but with a simple bow.

The second creature turned to walk away, but it stopped to say, "Oh, and I suggest you dispose of this first subject here. I expect you'll make far better hybrids with what you've learned from this one, making it obsolete by comparison. I see no point in keeping it. It would only prove to be a liability."

The first creature responded with a grunt, and the second creature left the way it came ... back into the shadow.

Then there was a crack.

I whipped my gaze toward the sound, and when my dad's body dropped, so did my heart. I'm glad I was in too much shock to scream, otherwise, that thing might have killed me, too. What did happen wasn't much better, but at least I'm alive.

The creature stood over my dad's body and used its single nostril to suck some kind of yellow gas from it. I couldn't bear to watch any longer. I retreated deeper into the cover of the wooden crates, praying for this to be some sick, messed-up dream.

I couldn't breathe—well, I could, but it was too fast, too sporadic, and I wasn't getting enough air. I was panicking ...

I was making noise.

The creature stepped behind the crates and glared at me with its piercing red eyes. Sharp claws extended from its shadowy hand, and it made a sound like a ferocious roar, but also, like a blood-curdling scream. I backed away, but there was a wall behind me. I was trapped. With lightning-fast speed, the creature swiped at me, and the pain I felt when I hit the ground was unimaginable.

I thought I was dead. At that moment, I *knew* I was dead ... But I wouldn't be telling this story if it ended here.

I wasn't dying—it felt like I was, but I wasn't. No, I was changing. The creature had left a wound on my right eye that burned like a raging fire, so much so that I barely noticed how hot the rest of me was. I was running an instant fever. My muscles tensed and grew larger, and my veins bulged, turning black like the night sky.

I wasn't dying, but sometimes, I wish I had. This was so much worse than death.

I stood, though I didn't want to. Words escaped my mouth, though I didn't speak them. The words coming from my mouth were deep and demonic; I sounded like those creatures. But I also sounded confused and afraid.

The words said, "Where am I? What is this?" I stared accusingly at my hands, at the black veins running down my arms ... but it wasn't me staring.

I approached the creature that attacked me, but I wasn't the one moving my legs. I had no control over my own body.

The demonic words left my mouth again. "What have you done to me?"

The creature eyed me, momentarily confused, then it extended its claws once more and struck. But the attack didn't hit me; I caught the creature's hand with my own. With my other hand, I struck the creature with a force that toppled it to the ground. I leaped on top of it, and it flailed and screamed as I gouged out its eyes with my thumbs. My hands were covered in the creature's black blood, dripping with the thick, ink-like substance. When my hand clenched into a fist, a shadow ripped from the wall and flowed toward me like some sort of shadowy river stream. The shadow solidified into a sharp spike, then it fell, impaling the creature's heart. The blood splattered all over my face.

I couldn't watch, but I did. I didn't want to, but I had to. I couldn't close my eyes. I had no control over anything. I was only fourteen, and somehow, my life had turned into a horror movie in less than an hour. I wanted out. None of this was real. I didn't believe it. I wouldn't.

I tried to move, to regain control, to do something. If I could just get back home and go to bed, I would wake up tomorrow, and everything would go back to normal. Mom wouldn't have left, Dad wouldn't be dead, I would never have seen any of the creatures I'd seen that night, and I could go back to playing video games like any other fourteen-year-old boy. But the more I struggled, the more strain I put myself in. It was like whatever was controlling my body, whoever's voice was coming out of my mouth, was actively fighting to keep me from regaining control. But I wouldn't give up, I couldn't, and soon, the strain was too great, and I passed out.

Chapter 1

My name is Alex Peterson, and I'm twenty-four years old. Ten years ago, my life was turned upside down, and as for what's happened between then and now ... well, I don't really know.

It feels like my life has only just started, like everything before is just something I read out of a book once. It doesn't feel like me. My life started just months ago when I woke up one morning, emerging from a shadowy spot on a building wall.

Here's what I do know: My dad was killed, though I don't know who killed him; my mother was abducted by some faceless, alien things; and I remember how she looked at me when she left. She said to me, "You always have a choice." I don't know why she said it, and I have no clue what she meant by it, but it's ironic because I must be the only guy on the planet who *doesn't* have a choice.

I have a scar on my right eye, one long line stretching from my forehead to my cheek. I don't know how I got it, but it's always there, looming over me, reminding me that "choices" are a privilege—a luxury. Not everybody gets them.

So now what? Well, with my parents gone and my little "problem," I've become homeless. I checked my old home; someone else is living there now. So I took to wandering for a bit, looking for food I could steal when I got hungry. I try to keep away from society—I don't want to endanger anyone—so eventually, my wandering led me to the sullied streets of Neetro City. Sure, there're a lot of people here, but it's easy to keep away from them if you stick to back alleys, and there's always something to steal in a city. It's a fine line between keeping my distance so as not to endanger anyone and keeping close enough to get the things I need to live.

I met a girl here. Christine Summers. She's also a homeless burglar and almost as complicated as I am. We get along, like, really well. It's kind of nice having her around, and I think I can keep her safe from my "problem." It's easier when it's just one person I have to distance myself from when it happens. I can keep her safe ... That's what I tell myself, at least.

So now you know where I'm at, and that brings us to the present. Christine and I are robbing a convenience store in the break of twilight. Christine only has one rule when it comes to burglary: Don't expose anything that can be tracked. She can be pretty paranoid, but we've never been caught, so maybe she's on to something. We wore black sneakers, black sweatpants tucked into the sneakers, and black shirts tucked into the sweatpants. We also had hats to cover our hair and ears, sunglasses to cover our eyes, gloves to cover our hands, and masks to cover our mouths. And if that weren't already an insane number of precautions, we also wore black hoodies with the hoods pulled over our heads to cover our necks (and cement the possibility of getting heat stroke). All that to prevent someone from finding a strand of hair or a fingerprint that could be linked to one of us. Like I said, she's paranoid. But who am I to judge? Hell, maybe I should be a little more paranoid.

We also had backpacks, which we used to stash all our stolen stuff—food, water, and anything else that might be useful out on the streets.

"Come on. Please," begged the store manager, intimidated by our appearance alone. "You're taking everything. I gotta eat. I got kids—a family."

We responded with silence, which is Christine's rule number one-point-five: Voices can be recognized, so don't say anything.

Christine and I looked at each other and nodded, silently agreeing that we were finished here. We zipped up our bags, flung them onto our backs, and ran out the door.

As we left, I heard the store manager yell, "Bastards! I hate this damn city!"

***

We arrived moments later. Nothing special, it's literally just some back alley, but it's home for us.

Christine took off her hood, hat, and sunglasses, revealing her brown eyes and curly, ginger hair. Then she took off her mask and gloves and massaged her freckled, olive-toned cheeks. I followed her lead, taking off my gear as well. We both threw our bags on the ground.

"Well," I said, "I'd say we did pretty well today."

"You're telling me," Christine responded, crouching and rummaging through the bags. "We should be stocked up on supplies for the next week or so."

"The guy in the store seemed pretty pissed, though."

"Oh, boo-hoo," she scoffed. "He'll probably just go home to a hot shower and a loving family anyway. We barely made a dent in his life. Trust me.

"Catch." She threw me one of our freshly stolen candy bars from the bag.

I fumbled slightly but still managed to catch it without looking like a complete idiot, and I would have been happy to ignore that little fumble had Christine not been eyeing the whole thing. "Almost," she said. "If you'd dropped that, Scar, I would have laughed my ass off." That's what I go by these days, *Scar*. *Alex* just doesn't feel right anymore. She does know my old name, though.

After pulling out a box of crackers from the bag, Christine approached me.

"Must your amusement always come at my expense?" I complained.

"'Fraid so." She kissed me, held it for a bit, then sat with her back against the building wall and ate her crackers.

She kisses me often, but she doesn't do labels, so we're strictly "not dating." Of course, I'm the complete opposite. I like to know where I'm at with people. Do I dare bring this up to her again? I might try to dance around it a bit. I've got time to kill.

I sat down next to her. She tilted the box of crackers to me, offering me some, but I declined and started on my candy bar.

"Remember when we first met?" I said.

She rolled her eyes. "Here we go again."

"You don't even know what I'm going to say."

"Oh, yes I do. You're gonna give me some bullshit about how noncommittal I am and how you 'like to know where you're at with people.'"

God, she knows me too well. "I don't see why that's so wrong."

"We're not 'normal people,' Scar. We're homeless burglars. That's a spontaneous life, and maybe I like the spontaneity. Besides, don't pretend you don't like when we kiss."

"Oh, no, I do. I just like it to make sense as well. This has been from day one."

"You act like people don't kiss when they first meet."

I stared at her blankly. "They don't."

"They do in Italy."

"Okay, A, that's on the cheeks, and I'm pretty sure that's an air kiss; and B, you're not Italian."

"I could be. My drunk-ass mother is white, so you never know. It's not my fault I don't know where she's from."

"Well, judging from the colour of your hair, you probably have Celtic ancestry."

"Wow, that's a stereotype." She feigned offence.

"No, a stereotype would be if I said your mom is Irish because she has a drinking problem. This is a likelihood."

"When did you become a genealogist?"

"I feel like we're getting off-topic here."

She sighed. "Caught that, did you? Look, you and I have been running for what seems like a long time. I ran away from home years ago because I *knew* that anything was better than staying in that house with my mom. And you, your parents died."

"Actually, only my dad died. My mom was abducted."

"If you say so." She never believed that, and I guess I couldn't blame her. You really had to have been there.

"And on top of that," she continued, "there's also your *other* problem. You and I aren't made for 'societal rules.' We're outcasts. We live by our own rules."

"And those rules have to be confusing?"

She kissed my cheek. "Only if you make it confusing."

I decided to give up the lost cause. Maybe she was right. Maybe I was just too concerned with structure.

She ran her thumb over my scar for a second, and her face fell. "It's been a while."

"It's random," I said robotically.

"Still. I can't help but think ..."

"What, that it won't happen again?" I was getting a bit snappy.

She stared at me. "That it might happen soon."

I looked away from her. "It's, uh, it's getting dark."

She understood my meaning. "Right. You know what that means." She got a lighter from her backpack. "Time to light some trash."

***

The chilly, nighttime air turned into a warm breeze as it passed through the fire we made from lit garbage. Christine and I sat close to it, and she showed me a map of Neetro City, pointing out where we were and where we needed to go.

"Okay, I'm thinking we head here." She pointed at a location on the map. "There should be a drugstore in the area, and we need soap for showers."

"We also need water for showers," I pointed out.

"I'm sure we can find a pond to splash around in."

"In the middle of the city? Hate to break it to you, but I'm sure any pond we find here will be full of bird crap."

She nudged me. "Don't be such a princess. If worse comes to worst, we can always just use someone else's shower. I'm an excellent lock picker."

"True," I agreed.

"Oh, and we need new masks. The ones we have are getting kind of funky."

I eyed the map. "This drugstore's pretty far away, though."

"Right. We'll have to relocate closer to the store—easier escape route. Let's get some sleep tonight, and we'll start walking in the morning."

"Sounds like a plan."

Christine folded up the map and returned it to her backpack.

We sat in silence for a moment, the only sound being the crackling from the fire. Then I chuckled.

"What's so funny?" asked Christine.

"Nothing. It's just ... we work so well together now."

She grinned. "Only because you listen to me now ... and stopped putting yourself in weird positions you know you can't handle. But, hey, don't feel bad. The first time's always a dud. It's great now."

"... I'm talking about the day we met. What the hell are you talking about?"

"The exact same thing in a way I know will make you uncomfortable." She smiled.

"Wow, you can be a real dick sometimes."

"Only sometimes? I strive to be a dick all the time. Twenty-four seven. Grade-A."

"Sounds cumbersome," I mumbled.

"Really, though, the same fricking store? You had to?"

"I didn't know you'd be there. I'd been wandering forever; I needed food. It was just the closest store around."

"You're just lucky we did run into each other. You were so green back then, you would have gotten caught in forty-eight seconds. Easily."

"Forty-eight seconds? Really? That's unnecessarily specific."

"That's being generous. I should have called the cops on you myself; it was so pathetic."

"Well, I'm sorry. Not everyone can be the great and terrible Dog Burglar." I mocked her ridiculous, self-appointed nickname.

"Hey, screw you! That's a wicked name."

"What even is a dog burglar?"

"That's the point. It's unique. Everybody else is a cat burglar, and I wanted to be something different."

"And you picked *dog* burglar. That's not outside-the-box thinking, Christine, that's box-adjacent thinking at best."

She looked at me. "Remind me, what was your nickname again?"

"Remind me," I retorted. "Who gave me that nickname in the first place?" That was when I accomplished the oh-so-difficult feat of shutting her up for a few seconds. "That's right, ladies and gentlemen, *Scar*, from the mind that brought you *Dog Burglar*."

She stared at me blankly. "You feel good now? Feel like a big man?"

"Yeah, actually. I'm pretty pleased with myself."

She yawned. "Well, I need some sleep. Enjoy the win, dickhead." She pulled her hood over her head for warmth.

"Goodnight, Puppy." She jammed her elbow into my side. "Ow, okay, I take it back."

"You shouldn't have pushed your luck."

"I know. Foolish idea."

She smiled. "'Night, you."

I pulled my hood over my head as well, and we both drifted to sleep.

Chapter 2

My eyes tore open, begging to escape a nightmare I could no longer remember. My heart raced. Sweat dripped from my head. I was panting. I couldn't breathe. All these things are symptoms of a panic attack, but that's not what this was. I could feel it, creeping in from the shadows. I could feel it creeping closer, taking over. Not yet, but soon. Soon, I'll be bestowed with the most terrifying power on the planet ... and it will only be used to harm people.

I glanced over at Christine. She was still asleep, peaceful. I had to go. I can't be near her when it happens.

Standing, I carefully inched away, trying not to wake her. But I was too flustered, and I tripped over an empty can of pop on the ground.

"What's wrong?" said Christine, rubbing her eyes. My stupid clumsiness woke her.

I just looked at her, and my expression said it all.

"Oh." Her face fell. "I knew it'd been too long."

I nodded, though my trembling may have engulfed it. "I have to go."

"Well, maybe I could come with you this time—help keep everyone safe."

"And who's going to keep you safe?"

"I can protect myself."

"No, not against this. I've told you before; this isn't me. It'll kill you, and I can't ... I won't let that happen."

She bit her lip. It looked like she was holding back tears, but I knew she was just suppressing her own stubbornness.

"Fine," she said. "Just ... please come back in one piece."

I put on a smile for her. "I'll try."

For a moment, we held each other's gaze. There was sadness in her eyes. With Christine, sometimes stubbornness and sadness were the same thing.

Slowly, I backed off, then I ran.

This was for the best.

I continued to run through the moonlit city streets, pushing through all the innocent city folk. I just had to go, far away from Christine, far away from everyone. There was a fire escape ahead that led to the roof of an abandoned building that hadn't been demolished yet. I remembered noticing it a few days ago. It'll have to do; I don't have much time left.

I scaled it quickly, my heart pumping faster than my legs, and when I finally reached the roof, my time was up.

I collapsed, my muscles growing tighter and larger. My veins blackened like a shiver down my spine. The scar on my right eye burned, turning red like it always does.

And now ... all I could do was watch.

Everything I do, everything I say, everything I am, isn't me. Not anymore. It's the other me, the scar, the monster.

"Again," I said, with a deep, demonic voice. "Why does he keep moving?" I looked out over the city, focusing on the luminous streets. "He's moved away from the last location but closer to the one before that. Interesting. It's as if he's wandering. He can't possibly know where he's going."

I chuckled darkly in my head—the only place where I still had control. The *other* me hasn't been able to figure out why Christine and I move around so often.

"I wonder," I said. "Do you wander because you think you can keep me away from the rest of your kind? You can't. This place is teeming with your kind; I can smell them. Besides, I'm the least of your problems. The rest are still here, working in the background. And when that work is finished, you'll beg for it to just be me here."

It says that a lot. I don't know who "the rest" are, but I can't even think about this getting worse.

My skin darkened, and I fused with the shadows beneath me, swimming through them, down the building wall and to the nearest populated area. I emerged at an intersection, and I could hear the heartbeats of innocent people pounding against my eardrums. None of them took much note of me—they're city people; they've got too much to worry about to notice others, even monsters. Slowly, I pulled my hood over my head and attacked.

This was the part I hated most. Gouging someone's eyes out, ramming a fist through someone else's skull, squeezing another person's neck until it collapsed, blood leaking between my fingers—it didn't matter; it all ended the same way. I stood over their mangled bodies and eagerly pressed my hands to their skin, draining their energy away. It was like I was absorbing the life out of them. It wasn't enough to rip these people apart, I had to drain them, too. The bodies dried up and turned pale, like they'd been dead for weeks.

The intersection was empty now. Most were dead, but some were lucky enough to see the commotion and run in a different direction. I hated that I knew that. I hated that I could smell who was alive and who was dead, hear who still had a heartbeat and whose heart had stopped. I hated that all the screaming didn't faze me in the slightest.

"It's not enough," I said demonically. "No matter how much I consume, it's never enough."

"Perhaps I can be of assistance," came another voice from behind. It sounded similar to how I sound now.

I grimaced, refusing to look behind. "I do not require your assistance."

"Are you sure?"

"Quite positive," I snapped.

The other voice made a disbelieving grunt. "You've made quite a mess here."

"Feeding," I informed curtly.

"You shouldn't make such a scene. It's best to stay hidden. You know what happened to the others in Dimension-002."

"Yes, but the hybrid isn't here, is she?"

"What happened there can happen again. You're a fool to think otherwise."

"The girl was a fluke. The likelihood of that being repeated is incalculable."

The other voice gave one short chuckle. "Ironic that you think so."

I gritted my teeth.

"What happened to you is proof that we are not infallible ... And I am sorry for your misfortune."

I laughed. "Sorry? Is that supposed to cure me?"

"No, research will."

"Are you saying that you've devised a cure?" My eyebrow rose.

There was hesitation in the other voice. "Not yet. Perhaps with your cooperation, we can return you to—"

"To my what, my original form? This is my original form. I was born with this feeble body. How can you possibly hope to cure me when you are too naive to understand what made me?"

"I'm listening," said the other voice slowly.

"Unlike you, I've had time to reflect upon my predicament. Your kind is too preoccupied with Project Hybrid, and so you fail to realize that the body in which I reside is the offspring of Project Hybrid's first test subject. The serum was given to the test subject at birth, and you foolishly allowed him to procreate later in life, coding the hybrid gene within the offspring, dormant until unlocked by the touch of your species." I chuckled. "You wish to speak of irony? In Dimension-002, your allies removed the girl's reproductive organs so that she could not birth an entire race of hybrids. Now that you finally have your hands on the data obtained from her, your incompetence has rendered your intentions moot. The hybrid's DNA and the DNA that ultimately created me are one and the same. This body is the only other pure-bred hybrid in existence. I am the girl's child, and your kind created me."

I grinned. I must have been pleased, the *other* me, like I was waiting to prove some point.

But the other voice responded calmly. "You refer to us as if you are not one of us."

"I do not wish to be allied with your pack of imbeciles. I stand alone. There's nothing you can do for me anyway."

"Careful," the other voice warned. "If you are not with us, then we will consider you our enemy, and you will be executed."

I smiled. "Go ahead. You can't destroy me."

There was a low, amused chuckle. "Very well. Your demise will come soon enough, I assure you, but not today. I have other matters to attend to."

"You sound frightened," I challenged.

But the other voice was not provoked. "Farewell, traitor."

"How do you even keep finding me?" I looked back but not enough to actually see who I was speaking to.

"We've tagged you, obviously. It would be unwise to allow a loose thread like yourself to wander around unchecked. We'll be seeing you."

I could hear footsteps. Whoever I was speaking to must be walking away. My fist clenched, and I plunged it into a neighbouring brick wall. The debris flowed from the hole I'd created like sand. Breathing heavily, I fused with the shadows and swam away.

***

The night pressed on, and as it did, more and more innocent souls fell to the monster within me. Thankfully, I only had to endure it for a few more hours, and then control of my body was returned to me. Exhausted and in pain, I stumbled back to the alley where Christine waited. When she spotted me, she ran to me and gave me a big hug.

"You're okay," she said. "I couldn't sleep knowing you were out there."

"Sorry," I mumbled.

"Don't be. It's not your fault." She clenched her hands, holding on to me tighter.

When I flinched, she let go. "Sorry." Then she got a good look at me, and her mouth gaped. "God, you're covered in blood. Here, sit down."

Christine helped me to the ground and propped me up against the building wall. She pulled out some disinfecting wipes from her bag and used them to clean the blood off my face.

"You might want to clean the blood off your arms first," I said lightly. "Should've thought twice before hugging me."

She smiled but didn't say anything. She was cleaning off some dried bits of blood on my cheek from earlier in the night.

"Can I ask you something?" She spoke quietly.

"Sure."

"What's it like, when you're out there like that?"

I didn't answer.

"You don't have to—"

"No, it's okay. It's ... terrifying. I can see what I'm doing, but I can't do anything about it. I feel like a predator. All those people ... I can smell them, how good they smell. Like I'm some sort of life-sucking vampire."

She grabbed another wipe from the bag and started on my arms. "And ... you're sure you can't—"

"I already told you; I can't control it."

"But you're still conscious, right? That has to mean something. Maybe you can ..."

"I've tried, Christine. I've tried to fight it, but it's stronger than I am. Fighting it used to weaken it, make me faint. Now, it barely notices I'm there."

"Do you think ... do you think it's still conscious now, like how you're conscious when it's in control?"

"No. No, I don't think so. Tonight, it seemed confused when it realized we'd moved again. I think it's just one way."

She was silent, thinking.

"There was something strange that happened, though," I said.

"What?"

"Someone was talking to me, but not *me*, the *other* me."

"Who?"

"I don't know. I never saw what they looked like, but I think whoever it was knows about me, knows what happened to me."

"What makes you say that?"

"They said they could help me, that they could find a cure if I cooperate."

"You or the *other* you?" Christine clarified.

"The *other* me. They weren't talking to me; they were talking to the thing inside me. And the *other* me said something about being the offspring of a girl from some place called Dimension-002."

"And you think it's your mom?"

"Maybe."

Christine bit her lip.

"I know you think she's dead, but I know what I saw that night. Maybe this is what happened to her."

Christine cleaned the blood off her arms and then put away the wipes. She rested her head on my shoulder to comfort me.

I replayed the night in my head, trying to find something I missed, trying to get more information. Then I stopped. "Wait a minute."

"What?" Christine looked up at me.

"When I was that monster, it sounded like I knew who I was talking to, like I'd met them before."

"Maybe you have," she said lightly.

"Well, what I mean is I didn't recognize the voice. I don't remember meeting anyone who knows about me. But the *other* me does."

"I thought you were conscious when it takes over."

"So did I."

Chapter 3

"Hey," Christine whispered, her warm hand touching my cheek.

I grunted sleepily. After last night, I really just wanted to sleep in.

"Scar, wake up." Christine's touch turned into a light tap.

"Five more minutes ... maybe ten," I mumbled.

"I already gave you five minutes. We have to get going."

Again, I grunted.

That's when Christine's touch turned into something much more painful. I awoke abruptly and rubbed my sore cheek. "Ow, what the hell was that for?"

"Sorry, I was trying to wake you up," she defended.

"By slapping me in the face? God, Christine."

"It worked, didn't it?" She folded her arms.

I continued to rub my cheek.

"Aw, did I hurt you?" If she hadn't said this sarcastically, I might have thought she actually felt sympathy, but Christine's pretty cold that way.

She pulled my hand away from my face and kissed my cheek. "There. Feel better now?"

"Not even close."

"Oh, shut up. You're such a baby." She smiled and threw me my backpack, which I caught with my gut and almost vomited.

"I swear this thing is heavier than before," I said.

"I packed it while you were asleep."

"With what, a bowling ball?"

She grinned. "Nope, just all your useless shit."

"Now, see, I know you're not talking about the trading cards we picked up last week."

"And the stupid holographic flask."

"Wow. All right, hater."

She rolled her eyes and grinned. "Just hurry up and put that on." She pointed to the backpack. "We've got to leave soon if we plan on getting to that drugstore by nightfall. Remember we've still got to set up once we get there."

"Yes, ma'am." I was still rubbing my cheek.

"Scar, for God's sake, it doesn't hurt that much."

"Oh yeah?" I challenged. "How about you come over here and let me slap your face? Then you can tell me how much it doesn't hurt."

"If you slap me, I'll draw a dick on your head while you're asleep," she said nonchalantly as she finished packing her own backpack.

"Okay, I think you and I should stop sleeping so close to each other. The fact that you barely have to stretch to reach my face and draw on it frankly terrifies me."

Christine smiled. "You're lucky my drawing skills aren't top-notch. If they were, I'd draw a whole fricking sexcapade on your forehead."

"Yep, definitely got to find a new place to sleep. You are not safe to be around unguarded."

Christine threw her backpack over her shoulder and grinned. "Come on, you. Let's make tracks."

***

We walked down the busy city streets, the sound of angry car horns assaulting our ears. This is Neetro City, after all; road rage is all the rage here. (Does that count as a pun? Either way, I should write that down. That was good).

At some point during our travels, Christine's head found its way to my shoulder and her arms wrapped around one of my own.

"You all right?" I asked her.

"Fine," she said. "Just lowering our chances of being recognized. Public displays of affection tend to make people uncomfortable. So if we're a little more intimate with each other, people might be inclined to look away."

Always an angle with her. It wouldn't be very "Christine" of her to admit that maybe she just wanted to be closer to me. But still, she was probably right. We may keep well covered up when we're mugging people, but our clothes could still be recognized.

I looked at her. Her eyes weren't really focused on anything. Her mind was elsewhere.

"You're not thinking about last night, are you?" I asked.

"I'm always thinking about that," she said matter-of-factly.

"I'm fine. Aside from your rude awakening, I slept most of it off."

"I don't know how. You only got a few hours. You were out most of the night."

"Look, I've had this problem forever."

"Six months?" she said, questioning my use of the word *forever*.

"Sure, but before then, I might as well have been in a coma. Point is, you get used to things fast."

"I'll never get used to that. And I don't know how you expect me to. We don't know a thing about it. What if one day you don't come back? What if you get stuck as the *other* you? And that other person who apparently knows about you, who the hell was that?"

"Look, Puppy—"

"Don't call me that. I'm being serious."

"So am I. If we fill our heads with all that worry, there won't be room left for anything else. Dissociation can be a good thing sometimes. Act like life is great, and maybe sometimes it will be."

I could tell she wasn't satisfied with that, but she didn't have the chance to say anything else. Out of nowhere, an explosion erupted from a nearby building. We weren't close enough to feel anything more than the warm air rushing by and an annoying ring in our ears, but Christine still instinctively yanked me into the nearest alleyway.

"What the hell was that?" I said, but she shushed me and pointed to what was happening.

Bystanders were running from the exploded building as five men exited it calmly. Four of the men were dressed in black and wearing ski masks to conceal their faces, but the fifth man didn't look nearly as presentable (if you could call black clothes and a ski mask presentable). The fifth man had a crazed look to him. His hair was scruffy and blond, and he wore a white vest that was stained with yellow blotches, but he held himself with confidence. He was in charge.

The fifth man laughed hysterically, and the sound sent a shiver down my spine. "Well, that was fun. Excellent job with the pyrotechnics, Clint."

"Thanks, boss," said one of the other men.

He laughed again and then turned to another one of his accomplices. "You, what's your name again?"

The man stuttered something in response, but we were too far away to hear. The rest of them were talking so loudly, like they were putting on a show.

"Joey," said the one in charge. "You're shaking, Joey. What's the matter? ... Speak up, Joey. Let the world hear you."

"Right. Uh, sorry, boss," said Joey. "I just ... Well, don't you think we should be more discreet? I mean, the cops will—"

The fifth man's cackle broke Joey's limited confidence. "'The cops,' he says. You hear that, Clint? Tell him what we think about cops, will you?"

"They're a waste of space, boss." He yelled it like a mantra.

"Bingo! Look, Joey. Cops, they're just followers. Sometimes, to get shit done, you've got to bend some rules, break 'em, reshape 'em. Right?"

Joey's trembling was swallowing his nod, and the sound of police sirens approaching was not helping things.

"Okay," the fifth man continued. "Joey, I understand. You're new; this stuff is hard for you. Do me a favour, would you? Hand me your gun."

Joey slipped him a gun carefully, but the fifth man took it like it was a toy, waving it around as he spoke.

"This is the perfect thing to teach the lesson," he said. "Do you know what I love about guns, Joey? ... Speak up, Joey. Let the masses hear you. You never know when someone important is in attendance."

"Yes, boss," said Joey. "No, boss, I don't know why you love guns."

"Attaboy, Joey. Speak with vigour. Speak without shame." He patted Joey on the back. "I like the unpredictability of a gun. If someone points a sword at you, you're pretty much dead, but a gun? A gun has variables. You don't know if it's loaded, if it'll jam, rubber bullets, metal bullets ... Exciting, isn't it, not knowing what comes next?"

He pointed the gun at Joey, and Joey flinched. "Whoa, what the hell are you doing!"

"There's the spark we're looking for. Yell, Joey, yell like you mean it."

"Boss, this ain't funny!"

"Everything's funny to someone. This is a lesson, Joey, so pay attention. You want something done, then you've got to learn that rules, laws, order; it's an illusion. You've got to break it to make it. One step at a time; everything is breakable. Even the laws of nature—someone had to make 'em so someone else could break 'em. Oh, come on, Joey, don't cry. Remember, guns are unpredictable, always unpredictable. But I know what result I'm hoping for because, honestly, I don't really like you very much."

Like a crack of thunder, the gun went off, and Joey dropped to the ground.

Soon afterward, two police cars arrived on the scene, sirens blaring. Four officers—two per car—got out of their vehicles and readied their weapons.

"Police!" one of them yelled. "Drop your weapons and stand down!"

Three of the men dropped their weapons and put up their hands, but the fifth man chucked his gun over his shoulder as if it meant nothing to him. "Took you long enough," he said. "NCPD response times get worse every time the damn phone rings."

"Hands behind your head," one of the officers demanded of the fifth man. All of them were focused on him; they didn't even care about the others.

The fifth man gladly complied but not without a strange remark. "One, two, three, four, Madam Time is at your door."

Cautiously, the officers approached and handcuffed the men without incident.

"Five, six, seven, eight, can't get her to cooperate," the fifth man continued.

"Quiet, you," said the officer who cuffed the fifth man.

"Oh, I'm sorry, officer. Is my dilemma bothering you?"

"You have the right to remain silent—which I highly suggest you exercise. Anything you say may be used in evidence in a court of law ..." The officer continued to read the man his rights.

As the other officers led the other men into the police cars, the fifth man said, "You're going to want to uncuff me, officer."

"Is that right?" said the officer in a deadpan tone as he started leading the fifth man to the car.

"I'm not done yet, and I've only met two of them. If you don't uncuff me now, there's only one other way this will end."

"Are you threatening an officer of the law?" the officer challenged.

Then that was the end of it. Out of nowhere, the fifth man broke free of the handcuffs and beat the officer into unconsciousness. The other officers responded with gunfire, but the man just avoided them, dancing around the bullets. He fought like ... like he had an *other* self as well. Before long, all four officers were beaten and knocked out.

The man smacked his own arm like a piece of faulty machinery. "Almost. I can't get this stupid thing to work properly. I'm still not fast enough. Though, the enhancements are enough to deal with the local police, so that's something. But not good enough to fix it. Not yet." He stared at his wrist, a watch maybe, I couldn't really see. It surprised me that he was still speaking as if he were talking to a large audience. "Madam Time is at your door, watching you forevermore." It looked like he was tapping buttons on his arm for a bit, then he just disappeared, like, into thin air. He was gone.

"What the hell just happened?" I said.

Christine shushed me and whispered, "Let's just go and pretend we weren't here. This doesn't concern us."

"I beg to differ," came a cool and calm voice.

As if all this wasn't strange enough, a man in a suit and sunglasses was standing in the alleyway with Christine and me. Had he been here all this time?

"Mind telling me what you're doing here?" said the man, folding his arms.

I could have thought up a million responses to give him, but I didn't dare. I knew Christine's rules: No talking. Don't get recognized. Don't get caught.

I looked at her for confirmation, and she shook her head subtly from side to side. That means not a peep. We both kept still and silent and just eyed the man carefully.

"Silence, huh?" said the man. "You see, that's not very smart. You two are the only people in the vicinity who saw what just went down and didn't try to run. Now you're trying to leave and keep tight-lipped about it. That kind of seems to me like you two might've had something to do with this."

We stayed silent. Christine nudged me discreetly, signalling for me to run when she does.

"Unfortunately, this is an important matter, and I can't afford to be wrong," the man continued. "So I'll have to bring you back to HQ for questioning."

The man stepped toward us, and Christine dashed from the alleyway. But I didn't get that opportunity. I couldn't move, I wanted to, but my body wouldn't listen. I was paralyzed. This wasn't my scar problem; this was something the man did. It had to be. He must have hit me with a tranquillizer or something.

With my blurring vision, I could see Christine running down the street. She looked back only once, her face fell, then she ran, and I blacked out.

Chapter 4

I blinked my eyes open. Everything was fuzzy, my thoughts, my vision. I tried to put my hand to my head to nurse a low-grade headache, but I couldn't move it. I was stuck, bound to a metal chair by metal cuffs coming out of the armrests and wrapping around my wrists.

It was bright here, wherever I was. It stung my eyes, made it hard to get my bearings. From what I could gather, I seemed to be sitting in a futuristic-looking room—the walls and floors were all a spotless white colour. There were rounded doors to the left and right. No doorknobs, but they were sleek and glossy like the rest of the room.

Someone stepped in front of me and cast enough of a shadow to make the brightness a little easier on my eyes. It was a man. In fact, it was the same man in the suit who was questioning me and Christine in the alleyway. He still had on sunglasses, too. That's how you know this room's too fricking bright.

"Welcome back," said the man, his arms folded.

I refrained from responding. Christine's words were forever forged in my mind: Don't talk, and you won't be recognized. Though, whether I was recognized or not didn't really change my situation here.

"Still not talking, huh?" the man said.

I kept my mouth shut, drifting my focus elsewhere. It looked like there was a huge TV monitor mounted on the wall behind the man, but this didn't look like the sort of place you'd watch a football game. Where was I? How did I get here?

"I see," the man continued. "Let me tell you how this is going to work, then. Until you start talking, you're going to remain seated in that chair. You won't be provided with food or beverages. Your choices are to talk or starve. And if that's not motivation enough for you, there are hidden cameras all over this room connected to turrets that will pop out of the walls and shoot on sight if you try anything. In case that's not clear: You try to escape, you try to attack me, you'll be shot."

I just stared at him.

"What's the matter? Don't believe me? Well, if all else fails"—he pulled out a gun from somewhere inside his suit—"I can always shoot you myself. It's in your best interest to cooperate."

Well, that got my attention. "What do you want to know?" I said reluctantly.

He grinned. "Let's start with your name."

"Scar."

"Your real name."

"That is my real name."

He eyed me suspiciously. "Your legal name is 'Scar'?"

"Is that a problem?" I challenged.

"It's a bit on the nose if you ask me, but whatever. Last name?"

"I don't have one."

"I said cooperate."

"I don't have one," I stressed. I had to give this guy as little information as possible so this wouldn't fall back on me when I figured out how I was going to get back to Christine.

He glared at me for a few seconds then moved on. "What were you doing hiding in the alleyway when the explosion occurred?"

"Hiding," I said satirically.

"Hiding from whom, the police?"

"No." Well, yes, but not because I caused the explosion. I'm just regularly involved in local burglaries. I should probably keep that to myself. "What are you getting at here? Because it sounds like you're trying to pin something on me that I didn't do. What would *you* do if a building randomly exploded next to you? You're telling me you wouldn't run and hide?"

"Well, Mister ... Scar, the police got a tip that the explosion was going to occur, and they cleared the area before pursuing the criminals responsible, yet you and that girl you were with still remained. That tells me that the two of you must have been part of the group responsible for the explosion."

"We weren't. And what the hell kind of leap in logic is that? There's no way the police cleared the area beforehand; there were tons of people there."

"They were planted. It was a big operation."

I don't know much about police operations in this city, but that seemed a little farfetched to me. But if it's true, and they cleared people out of the area … maybe the night before when I was away as a life-sucking monster, and Christine was hiding in the alleyway … maybe they missed the two homeless people still in the area.

"Look," I said, "I was just passing by. I don't have anything to do with anything."

"Is that right? Are you in that area often? Where do you live?"

The door on the right opened and saved me from having to come up with a response to that. It slid upward until I could no longer see it—just a door-shaped hole in the wall. Through it, a woman entered confidently, and the door slid back down behind her. She was dressed in black—a tidy blouse and straight-cut pants. Her skin was brown, and her hair was short and black, but it was just long enough to pull off a small, tightly bound ponytail. An emotionless expression was impressed upon her face.

The man bowed his head to her as she approached. "Director."

"Agent Johnson, your attendance is required in the Transport Room," she informed—almost commanded, actually. She had a sharp Australian accent.

"Of course, Director Agatha, but what about him?" The man motioned his head toward me without actually looking my way.

"I'll handle him. On your way now."

"Yes, ma'am." He left the room through the door on the left, and it closed behind him.

The woman turned to me. "All right, then, what's your name?"

"Scar," I answered.

"Last name?"

"Just Scar."

She smiled. "Very well. I imagine you'll fit in quite well here. Most of the field agents only have one name anyway."

"I'm sorry, 'fit in'? I'm not staying here. I don't even know where *here* is."

"I'm afraid you will be staying here, Mister Scar, for the foreseeable future. Frankly, it's either that or we terminate you. And as for where exactly you are, I'm afraid that much is classified."

What the hell have I gotten myself into? "Is there anything you can tell me that isn't classified?"

"That depends."

"On what?"

"On your willingness to cooperate."

"And if I'm not willing, you kill me?" I clarified.

"I'm afraid so. I know this all seems rather extreme, Mister Scar, but unfortunately, you seem to have found yourself in the wrong place at the wrong time, and there will be fatal consequences for that if you are not fully cooperative. You can liken it to stepping out into traffic whilst distracted by your phone. You may not have intended to do it, but you did, and now you must return to the footpath before a vehicle runs you over."

"And you're the footpath?"

She shrugged. "It isn't a perfect metaphor. Let's begin, shall we?"

"Do I have a choice?"

"Of course." She raised her eyebrows as if challenging me to try something unquestionably stupid. I just sat still, and she continued. "My name is Hilary Agatha, director of the Assassination Police Department or APD. We are a division of the Neetro City Police Department. Our job is to act as the wall between society and those who would seek to destroy it."

"Whoa, whoa, hold up," I interrupted. "You're the *Assassination* Police Department, as in you're all assassins?"

"Not all of us; the field workers are."

"So you, what, assassinate criminals?"

"*Dangerous* criminals. You see, Mister Scar, the world is filling up with people who can't be contained, people who cause too much damage to society for containment to make a difference."

"Okay, but you can't just kill criminals. That makes you no better than them."

She scoffed at me. "Yes, that's what they say, isn't it? Unfortunately, the real world is a great deal different."

"Sure. In the real world, we wipe out people we don't like, and that's how we achieve world peace."

"You've quite the propensity for sarcasm, Mister Scar." She nodded, as if considering what I'd said. "Perhaps you need a visual."

She walked to the massive monitor and placed her hand flat on the wall next to it. A green line swam up and down the area around her hand, and when the line vanished, the monitor switched on and displayed a picture of a man.

"This is August Quinton," the director explained. "Brilliant man, if not a bit extreme. He was a chemist who planned on using his expertise to create a disease that would wipe out humanity. He succeeded in creating the disease, but our agents got to him before he could distribute it. Both he and the disease were eliminated." The monitor changed to a picture of a woman. "This is Wendy Hearthrope. She was an extremely intelligent killer whom we could not contain. She had a remarkable propensity for escaping every single prison she was sent to. So, she was sent here, and we offered her a position in our department. She refused, and so we took care of her."

"Is that supposed to be a hint?" I asked dryly.

"If you'd like to take it as such. You find yourself now in a very similar situation to Ms. Hearthrope before you."

"Except I'm not a murderer," I argued.

She scrutinized me and said, "Perhaps." Then she moved on.

The monitor changed again, depicting some kind of green blob that remotely resembled a person.

I gasped. "What is that?"

"That is what happens when you try to alter human DNA without a bloody clue what you're doing. This *thing* was highly radioactive and posed a serious threat to the city. We had to put it down immediately."

"How come I've never heard of any of these people?"

"Because, Mister Scar, they are not the kinds of people we want the public to be aware of. Could you imagine the uproar if people knew just how often their entire way of life was endangered in a single week alone? They'd be scared stiff."

This APD didn't seem good to me at all. Killers who kill killers and call it justice. I had to figure a way out of here and find my way back to Christine, back to my life. Not to mention, if my *other* problem rears its ugly head in here, well, then they'll meet a real threat to society.

"Okay, so you assassinate dangerous criminals," I said. "Great. What do you want with me?"

"Well, you'll be dealing with some of our newer offenders—that is, after your training, of course."

"Training?" I blurted.

"Why, yes. Did you think you could do this job the way you are now?"

"Who said I wanted to be an assassin? I want out of this place, right now."

"I'm afraid I can't permit that. You already know too much. If you leave here now, I shall be forced to eliminate you."

"What the hell are you talking about? I only know too much because you guys knocked me out, brought me here, and told me all about the Assassins for Society."

"As I said, Mister Scar, wrong place, wrong time. I'm afraid you've just lucked out."

"That is bullshit! I did not cause that explosion, and I did not ask to be here."

"But you are here, Mister Scar. Regardless of what I've told you, your only options from the minute you entered this department were to work for us or be executed. We take the secrecy of this department very seriously, and I think you'll find that regular due process does not apply within these walls. The choice is yours, Mister Scar. Do you wish to comply?"

I fell silent for a second, mulling things over. "I guess I don't have a choice."

"Is that a *yes*?"

I sighed. "Yeah, fine." At least this way I'd still be alive. I could figure out how I was going to get out of here later.

"Disable turrets," said the director.

"Turrets disabled," answered a computerized voice.

The director then started mumbling to herself, like she was talking to someone with an earpiece, though I couldn't see one.

"Red," I caught her saying. "Report to the Recruitment Room. I have a new trainee for you."

She approached me and tapped a repetitive trill on the back of my chair with her fingers. Then I was released from the metal cuffs as they slid back into the armrests.

I stood up and rubbed my wrists. "Thanks."

"You're quite welcome. And remember," she looked me dead in the eye, "your life is in your own hands now."

I took that as a warning not to try and escape.

"Director," said a pale man entering from the door on the right.

He had a severe look to him with sharp, blue eyes. And he wore strange black clothing, almost like a skin-tight jumpsuit that covered every part of his body except his head. Even his hands were covered. I couldn't help feeling like it was alive somehow. Like, I swear I saw it move occasionally.

"Mister Scar," said the director. "This is Red. He will be your training agent."

"How you doing?" He offered his hand to shake.

"You want me to be honest?" I grinned, accepting his offer and shaking his hand. I'm glad to say his suit didn't feel alive. It felt kind of rubbery, actually.

"Mister Scar here quite enjoys his sarcasm," said the director to this "Red" guy. "Your favourite sort of person."

He rolled his eyes at me. "We'll beat that shit out of you soon."

"I wouldn't count on it," I said.

He nodded. "We'll see. Come with me. Let's get started."

Red walked toward the door on the left and waited. I looked at him and then at the director. She motioned with her eyes for me to follow him. I sighed and walked to the door.

"Good choice, Mister Scar," the director said. "I'm sure you'll do just fine here."

I followed the man through the door and into a huge, white corridor with other doors branching off of it.

"So, where are we going?" I asked.

"The Room." He refused to make eye contact with me.

"What's 'The Room'?" I tried to make it sound as mysterious as he unintentionally did.

"What the hell do you think it is?"

"Well, I imagine it's a room, but given you slapped a *the* in front of it, I'm assuming there's something special about this room."

"That's great. Assume that in your head."

I didn't answer. Clearly, he wasn't one for chitchat. As I followed him down the empty, white corridor, I found my thoughts drifting to Christine. Was she okay? How was I going to get back to her? Every door in this corridor looked the same. I couldn't even remember which one we came out of. But, you know, these guys must leave this place sometime. Maybe if I just go along with it until they show me how to get out of here, then I can figure out where I am and how to find Christine.

One of the adjacent doors suddenly opened. From it, a man in a lab coat exited, pushing a dolly holding a large, cylindrical, glass capsule. It looked like there was some sort of frozen body in it. It definitely wasn't human; it had pitch-black skin and claws. But it also looked kind of familiar.

"Sorry," said the man as he passed us and carted the body into another room.

"What was that?" I asked Red.

"A deceased extraterrestrial lifeform." He answered as if reading a report, seeming far more interested in this topic of conversation than anything previous. "We found it behind some building in the suburbs about a decade ago, and we've preserved its body so we can continue to run tests on it without it rotting. It's quite a complex organism. It's taken some time, but we're learning what we can from it. For instance, researching the toughness of its skin helped us to develop these suits." He pointed to his strange, skin-tight clothing.

I didn't respond to him. He said they found that thing behind a building in the suburbs ten years ago ... back when I was fourteen and had two alien encounters. I remembered now. That's how my dad died. It couldn't be, could it? Is that what happened to the alien that killed my dad?

"Uh, how many of those, uh, aliens did you find?" I asked.

"That one in particular? Just the one. But we deal with other species occasionally, though it's not really our division." He spoke as if the existence of alien life was common knowledge.

He went on a bit more about some "Extraterrestrial Department" and how they managed to keep that alien here, but I wasn't listening. It was starting to come back to me. There were two of them that night, and this place has one. What if the other one was still out there somewhere? Was that who I was talking to the night the *other* me took over? Maybe I needed to stay here. What if I could get some answers? I never really cared all that much before, but if the opportunity comes up, would I really not want to know ...?

Soon, we arrived at our destination. Red stood at the white door as it slid upward.

"Welcome to The Room," he said, entering.

With slight hesitation, I followed.

Chapter 5

Unlike the rest of the APD's headquarters, The Room was not nearly as futuristic looking. The floor, ceiling, and walls were all a bland, grey concrete. There was one wooden chair in the centre, cloaked in extremely dim light. This place looked like a basement cellar for torturing people.

"So, here's how this is going to work." Red placed his hands on his hips. "You will not leave this room until you are fully trained, however long that takes. You will be brought food and water if need be, but that's it."

"That rough, huh?" I commented. "Sounds like something I should bring up to Human Resources. Do you even have that here?"

"No," he said flatly.

"Oh, see, you should. That's how you keep systemic issues from seeping into the work environment."

"Are you done?" He stared at me, bored.

I threw my hands up and shrugged. "Just a suggestion."

He sighed. "Let's get started."

"What's first? You going to teach me some kind of secret martial arts?" I joked.

"Nope," he said shortly, ignoring my attempts at humour. "It doesn't matter how well you can fight; an attack that you can't see coming will always get the better of you."

"That is how the element of surprise works."

He continued to ignore my sarcasm. "The sixth sense is what many call it—a precognitive awareness, usually attuned to danger. I need you to develop one."

"Oh, sure, no problem. I'll just pick one up at the sixth-sense store."

He responded with his index finger pointed toward the wooden chair in the centre of the room.

"Are you asking me to sit? You do know that requires words, right? And, also, a *please* would be nice."

"I'm not asking you; I'm telling you." He folded his arms.

"All right, fine." I took a seat. "I get it; you're not a joker. Don't worry. I'll beat that shit into you soon."

He glared at me, noticing I'd used his own words against him, and from the look of the glare, it was possible I may live to regret that.

He stepped toward me and held out his hand, and the red fabric of a blindfold seemed to flow out of the fingertips of Red's suit until he was grasping the full blindfold in his hand.

"Put this on," he said, handing it to me.

"What for?" I wondered, putting it on anyway.

"Sight is the sense people rely on the most, yet it is also the most easily deceived. By taking away your sight, you'll be forced to improve your other senses, and that is how a sixth sense is developed."

Something cold trickled down my neck. I flinched; somehow the sensation felt sharper because I couldn't see. "What the hell was that?"

"Water," Red answered. "Small droplets of water will continue to drip on you in a specific pattern, which will alternate with a selection of other patterns. And the timing of that alteration will alternate in a pattern of its own, all to make sure that you can't predict when the water will drop."

"Okay, so ... why?" There was a hint of annoyance in my voice, but I meant for him to hear it. He didn't seem too concerned, though.

"The mind is always trying to predict what comes next. If it can't, it will still try, over and over. Those countless, failed attempts at precognition will sharpen your senses, make them develop faster."

As if on cue, the pattern of the water droplets suddenly changed, and I shivered.

"Okay," said Red. "You're all set, so I'll just be on my way."

"Wait, you're just going to leave?"

"Yep." I heard footsteps walking away from me.

"You know, this is a form of torture in China or something," I called after him. "Pretty sure I read that somewhere."

I was answered by the sound of a closing door.

***

Minute by minute, hour by hour, the time passed as I sat, shivering and drenched in cold water droplets. I really hoped this was all worth it, playing along with this just for the prospect of getting answers about my life. I must have been out of my mind ... Hopefully, Christine won't miss me too much.

It was nearly impossible to think properly with all this water slivering down my spine. This was definitely a form of torture. I was alone, I couldn't see, and my nervous system felt like it was being plucked like the strings of a harp. Oddly enough, though, every now and then, I'd flinch, like a shockwave shooting through my body. The flinch wasn't the odd part, though. It was like whipping forward after an emergency stop in a car. I guess it was more of a jolt than a flinch. I didn't just flinch forward either; I flinched in all different directions. Maybe I'm overthinking it. I'm being tortured with water droplets; of course I'm going to flinch.

***

Footsteps approached.

"Whaddup, Red," I greeted.

"Did you just say 'whaddup'?"

"Yep, that was the choice I made, and now I'm slightly regretting it. Am I done with this water torture thing now? I'm starting to get really cold … and wet."

"How did you even know I was here?" Red questioned.

"I heard you come in."

"How did you know that it was me specifically and not someone else?"

I hesitated. I had an answer to that, but I wasn't so sure I wanted to say it. "I, uh … I smelled you."

"You smelled me?"

"Yeah, I guess." I didn't have to be able to see to feel him glaring at me. "I mean, not in a weird way or anything. I just smelled your scent, I guess. Not that you smell bad, just, you know, like how dogs smell people. Or, no, scratch that. Not like a dog; that's weird."

"For God's sake, shut up."

The water droplets stopped, and Red removed the blindfold from my face.

"Looks like you've developed a sixth sense rather quickly." He seemed pretty satisfied.

"Are you sure? I don't feel like I have 'precognitive powers' or anything." My tone mocked the idea.

Red just pointed behind me.

I turned, and there were a bunch of metal arrows scattered on the floor.

"Arrows?" I said, puzzled. "I don't remember seeing those here before."

"I shot them at you while you were blindfolded," Red informed. "You avoided every single one without even knowing they were there."

"Wait, back up. You shot at me while I was blindfolded? Are you insane? Who does that?"

"I do, for training. It's gotten me good results so far."

"Ignoring the high injury rate, right?"

"Actually, trainees are more likely to die than be injured. I shoot to kill."

I swallowed.

Red's suit spawned a towel from his hand, the material flowing out of his fingertips. "Here, dry yourself off with this."

I stood from the chair and took the towel. "How do you keep making stuff appear from your suit?" I wondered.

"You'll get your own suit when you finish training. It'll be explained then."

"All right. Speaking of suits, can I get some dry clothes? The ones I'm wearing are drenched."

"You'll get new clothes when you get your suit. Until then, you'll wear the clothes you have."

"See, that's why this place needs a human resources department; your not giving me dry clothes feels like a human rights violation."

He ignored me and spawned a container of food and a water bottle from his suit. He handed them to me. "Eat. Drink. You'll need your strength."

I examined the white container. It had a transparent lid, and I could see some sort of grey sludge inside. When I opened the container, I wished my sense of smell hadn't improved. The scent was difficult to compare, but trust me, it was bad.

"What is this?" I asked, poking the lumpy sludge.

"That is a mixture of vitamins and nutrients—everything your body needs."

I tasted it. "Bleh! Everything except flavour. Haven't you ever heard of seasoning? I mean, is there even any salt in this?"

"There's some sodium in it, yeah."

"Not enough if you ask me," I grumbled.

***

My training continued over the next several weeks—some strength training, fighting-skills training, cognitive-resilience training—all things that made more sense than the sixth-sense thing did at first. I picked things up pretty quickly. It's not like I had anything else to focus on. I was also granted the privilege of showering when my stench became unbearable, but I still had to put on the same clothes afterward.

Now that I'd become fairly proficient at everything Red was teaching me, only one thing remained.

"Put these on," said Red.

We stood in the all-white room we'd been using for training (a fortunate upgrade from the torture chamber known as The Room), and he handed me two wristwatches with black straps and glowing green faces.

I put them on, one on each wrist. "What are these for?"

"Tap the faces, first right, then left."

I did so, and after tapping the left one, some sort of black goop swarmed out of the watch faces. I shook my hands instinctively, as it looked like a stream of ants crawling up my arms, but no matter how much I shook, I couldn't get it off ... It wasn't ants. The goop quickly covered every inch of my body except my neck and face. Then I understood.

"Is this my suit?" I sounded a little excited. I guess when you spend so long training, getting this suit was like getting a trophy.

"That is an External Nanobot Skin," he said. "It consists of tiny nanobots that will alter your body's functions as long as you are wearing it."

I looked at him blankly. "Which means?"

"It means that your body will function at superhuman levels."

I examined the black material covering my arms. I guess I did feel different, not exactly "superhuman" but different.

"The suit's nanobot material allows it to repair any structural damage you may suffer," Red continued. "Though, if you're wounded too much in too short a time, the suit will become overwhelmed and malfunction, so try not to get beaten up too badly. The suit can also sense if the atmosphere has become hazardous and will respond by covering your nose and mouth and filtering out toxins. And lastly, the suit is able to shrink down any substance and store it within the nanobots themselves."

"So that's how you're able to spawn stuff out of your suit, right?"

"Correct." He folded his arms. He seemed kind of satisfied.

"All right, cool. So is that all?"

"For suit functions, yes. Now I'll explain gadgets."

"Gadgets?" I said, sounding way more excited than I meant to.

Red looked at me cautiously. "Yes, gadgets. All of the suit's gadgets are thought-controlled, so to activate them, you'll just need to think of the name. You've got four gadgets in total. Number one: Claws." I thought of the name when he said it, and ten short, slightly curved, metallic talons emerged from my fingertips. "The Claws function in the way you'd expect. They are made out of an extremely strong mixture of metals from around the world. They will never rust, and they're even strong enough for you to grip onto a wall or ceiling. I don't recommend doing that often, though. It's very difficult to manoeuvre when you're clinging onto a wall."

"Uh, question," I interrupted, examining the Claws' sharpness.

"What?"

"How do I retract these things? I mean, they're cool and all, but knowing me, I'll probably accidentally scratch my own eyes out or something."

Only when I saw him staring at the scar on my face did I realize the irony in that. "They'll automatically retract after thirty seconds if you don't use them," he said. "That's the same for all your gadgets. But if you need to get rid of them quicker, just picture them retracting, and they will."

I nodded, carefully watching the Claws retract into the fingertips of my suit.

"Moving on," Red continued. "Number two: Sticky String." I activated the gadget with a thought, and two little tubes popped out of the back of my wrists, just before the watch faces. "The Sticky String is a super-adhesive thread capable of adhering to almost anything. It will fire and detach from your wrist at a mental command. It's also incredibly strong but not very resilient, so don't go swinging anything from it; we're not comic book characters."

"Could've fooled me," I mumbled.

He glared at me. "This is an official department of the Neetro City police."

"It sure is." I grinned. "And you name your gadgets *Claws* and *Sticky String*."

"The names are simplistic so that even a smart-ass like yourself can recall them when you need to."

"Ouch. Didn't know you had those sorts of comebacks in you."

He sighed. "Let's just get on with this. Number three: Tractor Palm." I activated the gadget, and my palms filled with a single green circle each. "The Tractor Palm works like an electromagnet. It can be used to push and pull magnetic objects without touching them. Its most practical use is to disarm someone."

Red stared at me expectantly.

"What?" I asked.

"This is usually when you butt in with some stupid remark."

"Oh, well, sorry to disappoint. I didn't think that one was worth a snide comment, given it's the only one so far that seems reasonable." He raised a brow at me, so I explained. "I mean, come on. Why would I need Sticky String and Claws? Is this a rodeo?"

He scoffed. "Look, maybe just consider for a second that you have no clue what sort of people threaten this city every day. The APD handles criminals who can't be handled. What do you think that means? Can you imagine the sort of people we go up against? Trust me when I say those gadgets with their silly names will save your life out in the field."

I was silent. What had I gotten myself into?

Red shook his head, sighed, and continued. "Number four: Visor." When I activated this gadget, the nanobots of the suit crawled toward my ears. From there, a pair of thick glasses materialized around my eyes. "Now, you can switch between modes of the Visor by tapping either side of it twice with your finger. There are three modes: Regular, X-ray, and Thermal. Regular is the default mode you'll be in upon activation of the Visor. It's essentially just a basic pair of glasses, but there are some useful features such as telescopic view, allowing you to 'zoom in' your vision, and access to the APD's database to help identify anything you see."

"So it'll let me know if the ugly creature across the street is actually a dog?"

He eyed me. "Hmph." I couldn't tell if that was a concealed chuckle or poorly veiled contempt. "The X-ray mode is as it sounds. It can be useful for revealing hidden weaponry. You'd be amazed at how often we come across people with dangerous, biological enhancements."

I tapped the side of the Visor to test it. The view switched like a camera shutter, and suddenly, I could see Red's skeleton. It didn't allow me to look through the walls, though. I guess that made sense. A secret organization probably isn't in the business of handing its agents the means to spy on them.

I nodded. "Cool. What's the last one do?"

"The last mode is Thermal, which will colour code everything you see based on heat signatures."

I activated it, and my vision was flooded with various hues of blue and red. Red and I had a lot more reds and oranges, whereas the walls and floors had more blues.

"Okay, cool," I said. "How is this useful, though?"

"Heat signatures can be a lot more useful for tracking than sight," he explained. "For instance, I once had to track a woman who had created an invisibility suit using an adaptive, light-reflective fabric."

"What'd she use it for, robbing banks?"

"Let's just say it's not much of an exaggeration to call her a succubus."

"She used it to have sex with people?"

"No, she used it to rape people," he corrected. He must have caught the expression on my face because he nodded knowingly. "Now you're starting to get it. Could you imagine not being able to catch a piece of shit like that? She was invisible, agile, and incredibly skilled at evasion. Most of her victims were men who didn't want to admit to being one of her victims, but the ones who did had trouble being believed. It didn't help that no one had ever seen this woman. All it took was one APD agent. I set my Visor to Thermal, found her easily, and brought her in."

"Then you killed her," I added with a raised brow.

"You'd rather I didn't?" he challenged. "If I kept her alive, she would have found a way to escape. She was good at that."

I found it difficult to argue with him. A lot of bad things happen in this city. It's not what I'd consider a very safe place; you definitely have to keep your guard up at all times. But how much crap happens in the city that I didn't even know about? How many people has the APD saved without anyone knowing it? They were all assassins, but maybe that's only because they had to be.

"And on that note," Red continued, "that's your training done."

"Really?"

"Enough to get you out into the field at least. You'll learn a lot on the job.

"Now, I'll show you to your new sleeping quarters, and you can get some rest."

"You mean I don't have to sleep on the floor anymore?"

"Not anymore. There'll be a change of clothes waiting for you when we get to your sleeping quarters." Thank God for that.

"Speaking of changing clothes," I said. "How do I get this suit off?"

"Tap the watch faces, left then right."

I did so, and the suit slivered back into the watch faces, revealing my black hoodie and sweatpants.

We walked out of the training room and down the futuristic-looking corridor until arriving at our destination. The white doorway slid upward, unveiling a small, white room with a single bed and a change of clothes upon it.

"Here you go," said Red. "I suggest you get as much sleep as you can. Trust me, you're going to need it."

"Thanks. I'll probably take a shower first, though."

He sniffed once. "That'd be best." Then he walked off and left me to my own affairs.

I headed for the showers first, got cleaned up, and then came back and entered my sleeping quarters. The door slid closed behind me. I ran my fingers against the walls; they were smooth and glossy, a lot different from the rough texture of The Room's walls.

I changed into the clothes left for me on the bed—nothing special, just a black vest and black pants.

I lay down on the bed and thought for a second. I'll have to do field work soon, and when that time comes, and they let me out of here, what am I going to do? I can't run; they'd catch me easily. Plus, there are things here that I need to find out about—that alien from my childhood. And I can't believe I'm saying this, but maybe these people aren't so bad. Maybe helping them would be a good thing. Maybe that's what my mom meant when she told me all those years ago that I always have a choice. I have the tools and training to help people, so maybe I should.

But what about Christine? How am I going to find her? Should I even try? The APD seems to love their secrecy; if I find Christine, and they find out, she'll be given the same options that I was: join or die. She can be a lot more stubborn than I am. I honestly don't know which one she'll pick. Maybe it would be better to just keep her out of this, just trust that she'll be fine and worry about my own situation.

And then, of course, there's my *other* problem. I suppose that's the biggest question of them all. What am I going to do when time runs out and the *other* me shows up?

Chapter 6

"**M**ister Scar," a voice called.

I rubbed my eyes, slowly awakening from my deep slumber.

"Mister Scar, report."

"What? Who said that?" I asked sleepily.

"This is Director Agatha," she answered.

I looked around my empty sleeping quarters. "Where are you?"

"Did Red not tell you? All wearers of an ENS are able to communicate with one another telepathically."

"ENS?"

"External Nanobot Skin. Honestly, didn't he teach you anything?"

"Sorry, recall's a little difficult when you're half asleep. What time is it anyway?"

"It is currently 2:47 a.m.," the director informed.

"Two forty-sev—okay, why the hell are you waking me up at two forty-seven in the morning?"

"To present you with your first mission, Mister Scar."

"Mission? You woke me up for a mission?"

"Indeed. Now, I'd like you to come to my current location. I'm sending it now."

"Sending what?"

"The directions. You'll be able to follow them with your Visor. Make haste, Mister Scar, over and out."

"Wait, hang on ..." There was a beep, and she was gone.

I sighed, got out of bed, and faced the futuristic look of the APD's headquarters.

"Okay," I said to myself. "I need the Visor, so I guess I'd better activate this stupid suit."

First right, then left, I tapped the watch faces. The nanobots scurried all over me like ants and formed the suit. Then I activated the Visor and immediately saw a notification on the lenses: "Activate directions?" I figured since everything else in this suit was thought-controlled, this must be, too. So I thought about activating the directions, and then the notification disappeared and was replaced with a green arrow leading out through the door. The door slid open as I walked through it, and a line of green arrows pointed left and down the corridor. I sighed and followed.

After a few turns, I arrived at my destination—the same room I was in when I'd first gotten here, the one with the big TV screen. The Visor displayed the words "Arrived at destination. Deactivate Visor?" I thought *yes*, and the Visor was deactivated.

Standing in front of the monitor was Director Agatha, sporting a nanobot suit of her own. There was also another woman, wearing a nanobot suit as well. She stood tall in the centre of the room and looked to have a doughy consistency to her skin. Her long, black hair was bone straight and ran down to her shoulders.

"Mister Scar," said the director. "This is Chloe. She will be joining you on your mission."

The woman approached and shook my hand. "Nice to meet you, Scar."

"Likewise," I replied.

"Well then," said the director. "You two had best be on your way."

"Right," said Chloe. She looked at me. "Follow me. I'll bring you up to speed on the way."

She exited the room swiftly, and I followed her into the white corridors.

"So," she began, "for your first mission we won't be doing anything too difficult, just stopping a bank robbery."

"That's it? You're not going to ask me to murder a crime lord or anything?"

She chuckled. That's new. I guess not everyone here has a stick up their ass. "Just because we're assassins, doesn't mean all we do is kill people. It only means we're *qualified* to kill people."

"Well, that is an important distinction."

She smiled. I could already tell I was going to get along with Chloe a lot better than I do with Red.

"Do you always wake up in the middle of the night for missions?" I asked her.

"Only the important ones, which this one definitely is. We've got seven armed robbers, each with a hostage. The police can't engage without threatening innocent lives, but we can."

We walked into a room, which housed a large cylindrical machine, stretching from floor to ceiling. It was glowing green, and a low humming sound radiated from it.

"Where are we?" I asked.

"The Transport Room," Chloe explained. "The whole city's divided into nineteen sectors. All we have to do is tell the Transporter where we're going, and we'll be transported to the nearest sector. Or, if you're not going anywhere specific, you can just name a sector, and the Transporter will take you to a general location there pre-designated by the APD."

"Uh-huh. And when you say transported, what do you mean exactly?"

She smiled. "I mean teleported."

"Doesn't that require getting destroyed and rebuilt someplace else? I'm sure I read that in a magazine or something."

"Wow, look at the big brain on you." She stepped over to me and clapped a hand on my shoulder. "Don't worry about it. You'll be fine. It's very sci-fi; you'll love it."

"If you say so. But if I get hurt, I'm totally suing you."

She laughed. "You can't sue an assassin, dumbass. We operate outside the law. If one of us gets out of line, you just send another assassin after them. Kill or be killed. So you'd better not piss me off." She grinned.

"Right. Wouldn't dream of it." My eyes darted away from her.

"You'll be fine, rookie. Don't sweat it." She faced the cylindrical machine. "Transporter, send Scar and me to the Bank of Neetro City."

A robotic voice answered. "Calculating. Transporting Agents Chloe and Scar to Sector Six. Do you wish to proceed?"

"Affirmative," Chloe authorized.

"Now beginning transportation."

"You might want to clench up, by the way," Chloe said to me. "The arrival can be a little rough sometimes."

Before I could respond with a witty comment, we were zapped with a green laser that shot down from the ceiling. For a fraction of a second, everything went black, then we were at our destination. Actually, we arrived on the rooftop of a neighbouring apartment building, about half a block away from the bank.

The Bank of Neetro City pierced the night with its luminous appearance. It stood tall and regally with grandiose front doors. It was the largest bank in the city, and it certainly looked the part.

"We've got to move," said Chloe, her black hair flowing in the wind like a silk sheet. "You ready?"

"Uh, no," I said. "Two questions first."

"Be quick about it." She smiled and sighed at the same time.

"Okay, first, if this is a bank robbery with hostages, where are all the cops?" The bank didn't look like it was housing a serious hostage situation at all. No police sirens, no cops guarding the exits.

"What do you mean 'where are all the cops?' We're the cops."

"We're cops?" My head tilted slightly.

"Not literally. I told you before; the cops can't do anything in this situation, so it's up to us."

"So the real cops don't even bother to show up? We're just supposed to deal with it?"

"Yes. Is that really what you want to get hung up on? We need to get down there; there's a robbery in progress. So I swear to God, if your next question is not actually pressing, you'd better hold it in."

"Actually, that leads into my next question nicely," I said. "Wouldn't it have made more sense to be dropped off closer to the bank, maybe on the bank's rooftop? How the hell are we supposed to get into the bank from here in a timely manner? I doubt the stairs are very fast."

"Oh, that's easy." She smiled. "Just use your wings."

"Wings? What wings?"

"The ones that sprout out of your back, obviously."

"What are you talking about?"

"Don't tell me you forgot them."

"Are you messing with me?"

"Maybe." She grinned, stepping toward the edge of the roof. "If you don't have wings, though, you'll have to do it the old-fashioned way."

"Which is?"

"Jump. Like this." Chloe leaped off the building.

Running over to the side of the roof, I witnessed her stick a perfect landing, completely unharmed.

I stood there, gawking down at her. I could barely keep my mouth shut. She just survived a drop from at least five storeys high.

"Yo, rookie." Chloe's voice sounded in my head due to the abilities of our suits. "Are you going to jump, or are you too busy shitting yourself?"

"Do I really have to answer that?"

"Just jump. The suit will compensate for your ... inexperience. Oh, and remember to bend your legs on the landing. And hurry it up, will you? We've got to go."

"All right, all right."

After taking a second to psych myself up a bit, I took a deep breath and jumped. Chloe was right. As I fell, I could feel the suit working to keep me balanced and making sure I didn't go into a tumble. It was like I was being gently guided, a loose autopilot. Of course, that did nothing for my general fear of life-threatening activities (the kind of fear any sensible person would have), and so I screamed. The suit responded to that by covering my mouth and blocking the sound coming out of it. I assumed this was in case I had to be stealthy or something, so my scream wouldn't blow my hypothetical cover.

I landed rather softly on the ground next to Chloe with bent knees.

"All good?" she asked.

I was still for a few seconds, waiting for a searing pain to tell me, *You just jumped off a fricking building; of course your legs are broken*, but no such pain occurred, so I said, "Yeah, guess so."

"All right, then." We started making our way to the bank, sticking to the shadows. "See those guys?" Chloe pointed toward two men who had just left the bank. They appeared to be armed with handguns equipped with silencers.

"Yeah," I replied.

"They're probably lookouts trying to figure out how much time they have before cops start showing up. I need you to take care of them while I scope out whatever's going on inside the bank. Got it?"

"Sure," I said hesitantly. She made it sound easy enough, and I did have the appropriate training for it, but those were still real criminals with real weapons.

"Good. Then get going. I'll meet up with you when you're done." She leaped out of sight. Where? I have no clue. I didn't even know these suits granted remarkable jumping ability, but I guess they do.

I made a stealthy approach toward the lookouts. How was I going to do this? Not looking as terrified as I felt was probably a good start. But then what? I could try and emulate that agent who first brought me to the APD. Or I could try to be like Red or even Chloe. Or ... maybe I should do this my way.

With a thought, I activated my Tractor Palms and hid against a shadow-shrouded part of the bank's wall. I raised my hand and pointed the Tractor Palm at one of the lookouts' guns.

"Here goes nothing," I muttered.

I used the Tractor Palm to magnetize the gun and nudged it into the other lookout. In effect, it looked like one of them had pushed the other.

"Watch it," the lookout whispered, pushing the man off of him.

"Sorry. My hand must've just twitched or something," said the other lookout.

"Dude, you're holding a gun. Keep that shit steady."

"Nah, nah, you're right, man. Won't happen again."

Well, that wasn't really the result I was looking for. Maybe if I do it again something more interesting will happen. I raised my hand and pushed one of them into the other again.

"I ain't playing with you, man," the lookout whispered harshly.

"I'm sorry. I didn't mean to," explained the other lookout. "I don't know what's happening. It's like my gun's got a mind of its own, man."

"I don't think you're taking this seriously."

"I swear I am. Honest."

"He may be taking it seriously," I butt in, "but I'm definitely not."

I stepped out of the shadows, and the lookouts stared at me blankly. Then they raised their guns and fired. A shiver ran down my spine—the sixth sense. It alerted me of the bullets coming my way before they'd even pulled the trigger, and my suit gave me acrobatic abilities far beyond human standards. Together, avoiding the barrage of bullets was simple, and soon enough, their guns were empty.

"Not into talking, huh?" I said to them. "You see a guy trying to strike up a conversation and try to kill him in less than a second. There really is no honour among thieves, is there?"

They ran to me, attempting to beat me unconscious, but I stood my ground and avoided every punch. Thanks to my training, this wasn't much of a fight. I just waited for an opening and knocked them out with a few well-placed hits.

"Just when things were starting to get fun, they fall asleep on me," I muttered. "Story of my life."

"Wow, good work, rookie," said Chloe, making a sudden reappearance.

"Were you watching?" I asked her.

"Just the last bit." She pointed up at the bank's glass roof. "I was up there having a look at things. There are definitely hostages we need to worry about, but the good news is that these guys aren't very smart. No one's guarding the entrance from the inside, and they're all too focused on the money they're trying to steal. They're not really paying attention to the hostages, and they won't be paying attention to us either if we take them out quickly." She sidled over to the bank entrance. "Follow me and do as I do."

We pushed open the large wooden doors and entered the bank.

There were seven hostages total, hands tied behind their backs and all lined up and lying face down in the middle of the bank's chequered, marble floor. As Chloe said, no one was guarding any of the hostages. The bank was pretty spacious and therefore echoey; maybe they thought they would hear it if anyone tried to escape. Definitely not very smart.

The people robbing the bank were all behind the teller's desk. They weren't even concealing their faces. These guys were asking to get caught. They looked to be planning their next move, at least until Chloe started on them, then they were pointing their big fancy guns at her, not that they came anywhere near close to hitting her. She leaped and dodged and knocked out most of the criminals before they even knew we were there. They were clearly inexperienced, and I wondered how they managed to get this far without being caught in the first place. But we still had to apprehend them quickly, just in case one of them decided that the hostages weren't so valuable anymore. I followed Chloe's lead, just like she told me to.

It wasn't long before the bank robbers had all been defeated, or so I thought. Out of the corner of my eye, I spotted one of them trying to escape through one of the bank's back exits.

"Uh, one of them's escaping," I pointed out to Chloe.

"Don't look at me; go after him," she ordered. "I'll get the hostages out of here. Go!"

With a nod, I obeyed her command and ran after the robber. He was fast. I followed him through the bank's back exit, into a back alley, and finally cornered him at a dead end.

"Going somewhere?" I said to him.

"Shit," he cursed under his breath, realizing he had nowhere to go.

He looked at me, fearful. "So, before I cart you off to jail," I said, "I've got to ask: What kind of person robs a bank and doesn't conceal their face? Seems pretty stupid if you ask me."

"Stupid ... or overconfident." The response didn't come from the robber but from a voice from behind. "That's just off the top of my head." There was a laugh.

I turned and looked at the familiar sight. It was a pale man, with blond hair and a stained white vest. I recognized him as the lunatic that Christine and I saw, the one that blew up that building a while back.

"I'm guessing you're running this bank robbery?" I said to him.

"God no," he answered. "I was just passing by."

"Passing by? In a back alley? Leading to a dead end?" I looked behind to visually confirm my statement. The bank robber was cowering with his back to the building wall.

"It's a free country, isn't it?" said the other guy. "No law against passing by."

"Well—" A shiver down my spine cut my sentence short. My sense of hearing sharpened abruptly, homing in on a specific noise. A ticking sound. Like a clock. Or ... a bomb!

Quickly, I activated my Sticky String gadget and shot it at the robber. It adhered to his shirt, and I yanked him over to me. Then I threw him over my shoulder and ran. I grabbed the other man, too, in my mad dash to escape the blast radius. I had only just made it to the front of the bank when a huge bang erupted. The force of the impact pushed me to the ground, and I dropped the guys I was carrying. It hurt, but my suit would heal me, so it didn't matter so much, as long as I wasn't dead.

I lifted my head off the ground. The air was warm and the whole bank was aflame. I could see Chloe leading the robbers and hostages out of the bank. Everyone seemed to be all right, and the cops had just started showing up to take away the robbers we'd just stopped. I guess they got called in to clean up once we'd dealt with the robbery. They probably don't need me right now. I can just take five, wait until my head stops spinning. Looks like the robber Chloe sent me after escaped in all the commotion anyway. I'll probably get in trouble for that.

"Well, that was entertaining," said the crazed man. He stood before me.

"You're still here?" I groaned. "This place is swarming with cops. I thought you would have run off like your friend."

"None of these idiots are my friends." He almost sounded offended. "Besides, I can't miss a chance to talk to you."

"What's so special about me?" I asked, head spinning too much to sound interested in the answer.

He laughed. "You're kidding, right? You're the third one. Not just the third one I've met but the actual third one. The last time it happened in order was ... well, it must have been centuries ago."

"What the hell are you talking about?"

He put a finger to his lips. "Shh, don't let her hear you." He chuckled to himself.

I thought back to the first time I'd seen this guy. I got the impression then that he had no regard for his own or anyone else's safety. It made me think. "Wait a second, did you plant this bomb and cause the bank to explode?"

I slowly came to my feet as he stood there pensively. "You know, I'm not sure." He took a huge, indulgent breath in. "It doesn't really smell like a bomb I would plant, but I did plant one around here recently for research. I set it for a random time, so anything's possible."

"Fancy meeting you here." It was Chloe. She was pretty good at popping in without being noticed. She stood with her arms folded, giving the man a killer stare.

"Do I know you?" the man questioned.

"What, you don't remember me?"

"Not particularly." The man scratched his head.

"Aw, I'm disappointed. After you broke out of prison, I was tasked with tracking you down. I thought we'd run into each other enough times for you to at least remember my face."

He squinted at her. "Your name's not Angela, is it?"

"No," she responded blankly.

"Thought not, then you wouldn't be with him." He looked at me.

"Mind telling me what you're doing here?" Chloe pressed. "You wouldn't be making it easy for us, would you?" The question was rhetorical.

The man smiled. "I was taking a stroll, thinking about … things. How long have you known him?" He pointed at me.

"I'll ask the questions," Chloe asserted.

"Oh, come on. I won't tell. Just us girls here. Well … and him." He looked at me again.

"What the hell are you talking about? You're a guy, too," I said.

He looked down at himself and seemed genuinely shocked. "So I am. Sorry. Sometimes it's hard to keep things straight in the old noggin. I've played a lot of different roles over the years, but I haven't been a girl since … well, probably since this thing broke." He pointed to a shiny wristwatch he was wearing. "See, lady?" he looked at Chloe, "I can share. But the look on your face tells me you're not going to reciprocate, so if you don't mind."

He started to walk away, but Chloe stepped over to him and grabbed his wrist. "I don't think so."

"I wouldn't do that if I were you." He grinned.

Chloe ignored the warning, grabbing his other wrist. That was a mistake. A force that looked to come from the man's body pushed her back, almost like a shockwave. It wasn't strong enough to harm me, but it did push Chloe to the ground.

"I did warn you," the man said. "Now, lots to do."

"Leaving so soon, Mirror-Mind?" Chloe said, coming to her feet.

"Don't call me that," he responded quietly.

"I thought you liked that name," Chloe teased.

"The name born from the idea that I am insane? No. I'm not insane, I don't have a split personality, and I don't see things that aren't there; I'm just stressed. I have a lot on my mind."

"Oh, you do, do you?"

He looked at me and then at Chloe. "More than you know. Anyway, I didn't rob this bank, so you don't need me here."

Chloe laughed. "Oh, I beg to differ. You're coming with us."

"Excuse me?"

"There's plenty of shit we have on you."

"Such as?" He raised an eyebrow.

"Does the possession and use of biological weaponry sound familiar to you? Or what about the murder of eighteen police officers? Or there was the time you blew up a hospital to escape captivity."

He smiled nervously. "You don't understand what I'm up against. How could you? No, you're too new. You haven't been touched by her effects, not enough."

"What are you talking about?" I asked.

"Time. In the end, she's everyone's enemy ... But you wouldn't understand."

"I understand better than you think," said Chloe, staring at him intensely. "You're an anarchist. You can make up any excuse you want to justify what you do, but you're an agent of chaos, Kennedy. You kill and you destroy because it creates chaos, and I think you like that."

He laughed. "I'm no agent of chaos. I'm just someone who needs to know. I push the boundaries because I need to know the precise point at which it will all snap!" He rubbed his face, trying to calm himself down. "I lived by her rules for a long time, learned them. Now I have to bend them, break 'em … see how far she'll let me go."

"Is that so, Mirror-Mind?" Chloe smiled.

"Don't call me that!"

She jumped into the air before the man even threw his punch. With a midair flip, she landed with a handstand perched on his shoulders and then shifted her weight until he toppled to the ground. And somehow, after that insane display of acrobatics, she still managed to land on her feet.

She materialized a pair of handcuffs from her suit. "It's over, Kennedy."

"No, it isn't." He smiled. "Almost but not quite. I'm not done yet. I'm right smack in the middle. Besides, I still have to fix this." He tapped a finger on his broken wristwatch, and as he did, a red light began to flash from it. "Time." He laughed to himself, then he faded and disappeared.

"Damn it," Chloe sighed. "I thought if I pissed him off enough, I could goad him into staying to fight. I don't know how to catch a guy who can disappear."

"How did he even do that?" I wondered.

"The running theory is bodily enhancements, probably the same tech we used to teleport here, but he's found a way to shrink it down and have it on his person. And he doesn't seem to need designated sectors or a hub area like we do for the Transport Room; he just goes wherever he wants, and we can't trace him." She ran a hand through her hair. "Anyway, you all right?"

"Yeah, fine," I said.

"Good. Where's the guy I sent you after?"

"The bank robber? He, uh, he got away in all the commotion."

"Oh well. Six out of eight criminals isn't so bad."

"Sure."

We walked toward the police, where they were dealing with the hostages and bank robbers.

"Sorry, can we just go back to that Mirror-Mind guy for a second?" I asked.

Chloe smiled. "Yeah, he really sticks with you, doesn't he? His real name is Roderick Kennedy, and he's currently at the top of the APD's hit list."

"Why?"

"The short answer: He's insane, dangerous, and has killed a ton of people."

"Sure, I can see that. But why does he have to die? Why can't we put him in an asylum or something? Give him some structure, a good doctor ... he might turn his life around."

She almost laughed at me. "That's cute, but we're not in the business of helping people. We get rid of people who are too dangerous to live. That man has broken out of every prison he's been to, and in the time it takes for someone to be lucky enough to catch him again—the damage and death he causes in the meantime—it's not worth it. He has to be stopped."

I thought back to when I'd first seen him, when I was with Christine in that alleyway. "I guess I can see your point. And what's with the name *Mirror-Mind*?"

"It's something the general public came up with. I think it was first said on the local news or something. It's a comment on his mental state—how he seems to talk about utter nonsense but does so in a coherent way. Like there's some sort of contrast in his mind."

"Sounds a bit aggrandizing," I commented.

"Yeah, a bit. And glorifying. But that's people for you; slap a silly name on someone you don't like, and it makes it easier to dehumanize them." She sighed.

"You all right?" I asked.

"Yeah, fine." She watched the hostages being questioned by the police officers. "I just can't help thinking that society failed men like him, you know? By the time the APD has to deal with people, it's already too late. When I was young, I was a bit of a troublemaker. I liked to push people's buttons and test boundaries, but I came from a rich family who wouldn't hear of it. I wasn't to speak unless spoken to. I wasn't to look anyone in the eye unless my attention was requested. I lived in a huge mansion, but I wasn't allowed to explore it. I was to remain in my room and only leave if called upon ... I broke every one of those rules, and I got punished for it all the time. I felt suppressed, like I was bad no matter what I did. And I bet, if I hadn't run away, maybe I would've turned out just as bad as Kennedy. Your childhood can really shape your worldview, and I always wonder what shaped his." She looked at me. "Look, I know you feel weird about all this, killing killers and such. The APD found me on the streets years ago, and I thought the same thing. But until someone figures out a way to stop people from getting to the point where the APD has to deal with them, we'll be needed. What we do isn't the best, but it's the best we've got to deal with a problem that's worse. Some people just can't be reformed."

I nodded. "I guess I can see that." I think I was starting to get it. It's not the APD's fault that this is the world we live in. They're just trying to do good the best way they can. And if they can get someone like Mirror-Mind off the streets—someone who kills and destroys without an ounce of remorse—are they really all that bad?

"Anyway, that's us done here," said Chloe. "Time to head back. You did good, rookie."

"Thanks ... Uh, this wouldn't have been a test, would it?"

She grinned. "What makes you say that?"

"Just the general competency level of those bank robbers. It just seems like the perfect 'rookie' mission."

She chuckled. "It was real if that's what you're wondering, and I didn't know Kennedy would show up, but yes, this was a specially selected mission for a rookie."

I smiled. "Thought so."

Chloe rolled her eyes and then spoke into her wrist. "Transporter, send me and Scar back to HQ."

A robotic voice sounded in my head. "Of course. Transporting Agents Chloe and Scar to the APD headquarters. Please stand by."

The nanobots in our suits started crawling up our necks, covering our faces. Chloe didn't flinch so neither did I. The suits made a slight humming sound, and then the transportation commenced.

Chapter 7

So, let me catch you up. The past few months have been a pretty bad time to be an assassin. That is to say, there's been no one to assassinate. (I suppose that's a good thing, all things considered.) That doesn't mean we're not busy, though. Mirror-Mind hasn't been sighted since the bank bombing, and because we can't track him, all we can do is wait until he pops back up. On top of that, there are two new threats that are keeping us occupied. The first is someone who has taken a liking to kidnapping people, specifically people over eighteen who've had children. And there have been no witnesses aside from some people saying they saw "a cloaked figure." The media seems to like them, though, whoever they are. They've dubbed the person The Adultnapper. (I wonder who got fired coming up with that name.) The second major concern is someone who's been supplying criminals with power-enhancing suits, bringing them to superhuman levels of strength. And that makes them too much for the regular police department to handle, which means they're the APD's problem. So we've all got our hands full with that. Whether or not we'll have to kill any of them remains to be seen. For now, we just have to keep things under control.

Anyway, here I sit, atop the roof of a tall city building, looking over the busy streets in the cloak of night. According to the sound of police sirens blaring in my ears, it was time to get to work.

Down the street, there was a speeding car being tailed by the cops—a classic car chase. Is it bad to say that I was actually kind of excited? I've been messing around with my suit's gadgets, trying to figure out some cool tricks I can do with them, and today is the first time I can put one of them into practice.

Using my enhanced senses to properly time everything, I leaped off the building. Activating my Tractor Palm gadget while free-falling, I faced my palms toward the ground and shot myself up about ten feet higher. With the extra height, I could reach a streetlight from which I swung and landed directly on top of the speeding car.

"Whoa, guys, did you see what I just did?" I said to the two people in the car, using my Claws to hold onto the car's roof as I poked my head through the open window.

"What the hell?" the driver replied.

"I just used the electromagnetic tech in my Tractor Palms to repel myself from the Earth's magnetic field, giving me a second jump. Like double jumps in video games."

"What the shit? Man, who the hell are you?"

"Look, I feel like you guys are way less excited about this than you should be. What I just did was awesome. Don't take that away from me."

"Jackson, get the shotgun and blow this son of a bitch off our roof," said the driver to the man sitting next to him.

"Is the violence really necessary? I'm literally just popping in; there is no need to blow my head off. I mean, who even raised you to ...? Hang on, did you say *shotgun*?"

"Yeah," said the other man, loading the weapon. "Shotgun."

He aimed and fired, but I was hit by something else first, a violent shiver down my spine telling me to avoid the shot before it was fired. I moved to the back of the speeding car. Though the shot missed me, it did just fire out into traffic. Cars swerved; people ran—I had to stop this quick.

"Are you insane?" I said, poking my head through the open window on the other side of the car. "You could have killed someone ... actually, I think you did kill someone. What's wrong with you?"

The man hastily tried to reload the gun, but I reached my hand through the window and crushed the gun barrel with my grip. He was shocked for a second, but he shook it off and readied his aim anyway.

"Oh, come on. Don't be stupid," I said. "If you fire that thing, it'll blow up."

"Yeah, and you along with it," he retorted.

With unperceivable speed, I punched the man and instantly knocked him out.

"All right, well, he's an idiot. What about you?" I directed my attention to the driver. "You want to stop the car and talk or—"

"Get off my damn car, you hooligan!" The driver took his hands off the wheel, grabbed the shotgun, and tried to spear me off the car.

It was easy for me to avoid his lunges, but the shiver down my spine had me concerned about something else. "So listen, I don't know about you, but I kind of value my life, and I'd really appreciate it if you would put your hands back on the wheel and keep your eyes on the road."

He ignored me and continued to lunge the shotgun at me like a makeshift spear.

"I'm serious," I cautioned. "You're about to crash."

He still refused to listen.

"Look at the road." I repeated it louder and louder as the danger got closer and closer. "Look at the road. The road. Please, look at it. Look at the—"

"What about the goddamn—" Finally, he looked and muttered, "Oh, shit."

I leaped off the car just before it collided with a lamppost. Executing a perfect three-point landing (which could probably earn me a place in professional gymnastics if body-enhancing suits were allowed), I witnessed the driver fleeing the smoking vehicle with a stuffed pillowcase in hand.

"Oh yeah, no, don't worry about your friend in the car," I called out to him (not that he stopped to listen). "You just keep running. Save yourself. I'll worry about getting your friend out of the car that could explode at any minute."

I rolled my eyes and leaped toward the car using the Tractor Palm trick I'd used before, landing on the hood with urgency. The air was starting to smell more and more like gasoline. Luckily, all the city folk had enough sense to start running when a car tore through the street and crashed, so I only had to worry about this one guy. I used my Claws to stick my fingers into the metal of the car door and tear it off. I dragged the man out and threw him over my shoulder, leaping far away from the car.

The car burst into flames as I cuffed the man to a streetlight. It's weird, I never would have imagined that assassins would need handcuffs, but it's a good thing this suit is stockpiled with them. The man was still out cold. He'll be a nice present for the police when they swarm in. In the meantime, I should go look for this guy's friend. There couldn't have been anything legal in that pillowcase he was tugging around.

I leaped over to a building and, using my Claws, latched my fingers into the brick wall and climbed to the top so I could have a good look at my surroundings and a better chance at finding the driver. And find him I did. He was running through some back alleys, trying to avoid the streets. After leaping to a few other rooftops to catch up with him, I returned to the ground and cut him off.

"Going somewhere?" I smirked.

He didn't respond. However, sweat dripped from his forehead.

"What's in the pillowcase? No, wait, let me guess. Is it money? Drugs?"

He remained silent.

"Come on, you and I both know you're not lugging around dirty laundry."

He trembled.

"Okay, tell you what, let's make this easy. You don't have to tell me anything. I'll cuff you and bring you to the police, and you can yell something along the lines of 'Dang it, you got me again, copper!' I don't know; I'll let you have fun with the line. What do you say?"

This time the man did respond. "You assholes can't push me around no more." He chuckled nervously. "I've got a secret weapon."

I folded my arms. "You do, do you? Let me guess, a Power Suit. Just like the other eighteen guys I've fought with Power Suits so far. I swear these things must be on sale or something."

His suit activated. The electricity that surged within it burned through the shirt he wore over it. For some reason, these suits seemed to have that effect. Whenever they come into contact with clothing, there's a spark of electricity, and the clothes burn off. But when they're not in contact with clothing, they just look like a grey, skin-tight shirt.

"You won't be laughing anymore," he said, dropping the pillowcase on the ground.

I raised an eyebrow. "We'll see."

He punched, I dodged, and that continued for a little bit. There was no way he was actually going to hit me; I was just waiting for him to realize that.

I shifted slightly to the side, letting his fist breeze right past my head. "You know, I was getting a little warm. I appreciate you fanning me," I taunted.

I kept dancing around his punches until I was backed up against the side of a building. He smirked and threw another punch, which went straight through the brick wall when I avoided it.

"Wow, you really showed that wall," I joked. "Give up yet?"

He threw a punch with his other hand, and it was just more of the same. What was it they say about insanity again?

The man tugged, but his hands remained stuck in the wall.

"So," I said. "As it stands, you haven't landed a single hit on me and now both your hands are stuck in the wall. Ready to give up now, or do you want to see if you can kick me?"

"Man, shut up!" he yelled. "Just take me to the police."

"Good answer." I helped yank his hands out of the wall and cuffed them with a special pair of handcuffs used for people with enhanced strength. Then I picked up the pillowcase (it was money), and I returned him to where I'd left his friend.

The police were there, just as I'd anticipated. They already had the first criminal in the back of a police car. One of the officers approached me and took the other guy off my hands.

"Thanks for your help," said the cop as he handed the guy off to a different officer who began reading him his rights.

"No problem," I said. "I needed a workout anyway, plus I was in the neighbourhood, so ..."

"Well, my hat's off to you, sir. Ever since these bastards started getting them Power Suits, they've been a lot harder to handle."

"Well, hey, we're all just doing our jobs, right? Trying to keep the city safe."

He smiled. "Guess so, yeah. You're with the APD, right?"

"Yep."

He looked a little starstruck. "I've never seen one of youse before. I mean, all us cops are told about this secret department but ... nice to finally put a face to the faceless, you know? What's it like, dealing with your kind of criminals?"

"I don't know. I'm kind of new, so I haven't really dealt with many of *those* kinds of criminals. I've mostly been focused on taking down people with these Power Suits."

The officer nodded. "Fair enough. You don't happen to have any info on where those suits are coming from, do you?"

"Sorry, no. That's actually why I'm out here. I'm looking for anything that might lead us to the source of these suits."

"I can only hope someone finds out soon. There ain't enough of you guys out here to help us regular cops take down all the yahoos with the suits. They'll have to start giving all of us suits to handle them."

I grinned. "I don't think the Neetro City folk pay enough in taxes to fund that."

He laughed once. "You're probably right. Well, good luck to you."

"Yeah, you too."

The cop returned to his police car, and I returned to the rooftops. Leaping from building to building, I felt uneasy. When I joined the APD, they told me how much crime ran through this city, and then I experienced some of that firsthand. But now the city's gone quiet. Not quiet as in peaceful, more like the calm before the storm, like something big is about to happen. Guess I can't stay a rookie forever. Sooner or later, I'll have to be tested.

Funny how in just a few months, this has become my new life. I guess I'm good at that—assimilating. I haven't thought much about Christine lately. I don't know if that's because I'm protecting her from the APD or if I just don't want to face the possibility that I might have hurt her by leaving. I mean, it wasn't really my fault, and she was on her own before she met me. How is this any different? I'm sure she'll be fine.

And then there's something else I've avoided thinking about. My *other* problem … And I think, for now, I'm going to continue avoiding it.

"Help!" I heard a woman scream.

I quickly matched a visual to the sound and confirmed that a woman was being mugged in a secluded area behind a building. Leaping from the rooftops, I landed quietly nearby. Unfortunately, that meant they didn't notice me drop in (pun intended). Perhaps I should introduce myself.

"Give me the money, lady. I ain't got all day," said the woman pointing a gun at the other woman. She wore a skin-tight shirt that looked a lot like the Power Suits all these criminals have, but this one was brown. First time I've seen colour options with these things.

"Money, huh?" I said. "What an original thing to steal. Don't think I've ever heard that one before."

The mugger turned to me with her gun ready. "You're in the wrong place, buddy. You better get up outta here."

"You mean this isn't the Neetro City Carnival? Man, I took two buses and a cab to get here."

"I'm serious." She steadied her gun. "Beat it."

"Beat it, huh? Well, aren't you a smooth criminal."

"Last chance."

What a wasted reference. That went clean over her head.

I glanced over at the other woman. She was too scared to move, but it looked like she was happy to not have the gun pointed at her anymore. "You don't seriously think you can hit me with that, do you?" I said to the mugger.

"Keep talking and maybe you'll find out."

"Keep talking? Oh, whatever should I talk about? Should I comment on your tacky haircut or your poor posture?"

That did it. She wildly fired her gun until it was empty. Not a single bullet hit me, obviously. "My god," I said. "You must waste a fortune in bullets. No wonder you need money. Have you ever considered target practice?"

"Man, screw you!" With gritted teeth, the woman pulled a knife from her pocket and rushed me.

"Ah, a knife, good choice," I joked. "It won't cost you any money for your lack of skill."

I dodged her knife swipes, making sure to mock her with my movements. I could have kept this going longer, but I could see the other woman. She was petrified. This wasn't as run-of-the-mill for her as it was for me.

"Well, it's been fun," I said to the mugger, "but it's almost my bedtime, so I think I'm going to wrap this up." I (gently) beat the woman into submission and seated her against a wall. She wasn't going anywhere.

"You all right?" I asked the other woman.

She forced a nod. "Th-thank you."

"No problem." I shrugged.

She looked quickly at the unconscious mugger.

"She's out cold," I assured her. "Sorry I took so long. I like to have fun with them first." I grinned.

She studied me. "Who are you?"

"Who am I? Uh, Scar ... I guess." It's probably fine to tell her that. I know the APD is supposed to be a secret department, but we don't have to stay in the shadows all the time; we just don't tell people what we are exactly. Besides, *Scar* isn't even my legal name.

Even still, she repeated the name under her breath.

"Listen, you'd better get back to whatever you were doing. I'll deal with this idiot," I said, pointing at the mugger.

"Yeah. Thanks again." She started off on her way.

"All right, back to you." I returned my attention to the mugger, who was starting to stir. "I wouldn't bother moving. I'm going to call the cops to come pick you up, so just sit tight, okay?"

All I got in response was a grunt.

"What's the matter? Don't want to talk anymore?"

No reply.

"All right, then. I'll just talk to myself. Let's start with your shirt. It *could* just be a regular athletic shirt, but I'm guessing it's a Power Suit. Everyone else seems to have one, and you wanted to get in on a good thing. I get it.

Question is: Why is yours brown and not grey like the rest?" I examined her suit. It wasn't just the colour that was different; there were also yellow streaks on the sides, for design purposes, I assumed. I also noticed two letters inscribed on the top-right. "DB? What does DB stand for?"

The mugger was silent.

"Hey, Madam Criminal, I'm talking to you. What's DB stand for?"

I think she tried to spit at me, but all she ended up doing was drooling all over herself.

"Okay, then." I went back to talking to myself. "It's not the most enlightening news, but I'd better call it in." Using my suit's communication function, I contacted Red. "How's it going, Red?"

"What do you want, Scar? I'm busy."

"Hello to you, too."

"I swear to God, if you're calling me again just to check that your suit's communications work—"

"No, no, no, I've got a reason. I found a woman wearing what I think is a brown and yellow Power Suit. Though, she used a gun, so I didn't really see if she displayed any enhanced strength. It could just be a shirt."

"Let's assume it's the former, just to be safe. Have you noticed anything else, any abilities that the other Power Suits don't have?"

"Not really. But it does have the letters DB inscribed into the top-right side of it."

“DB?”

“Yeah. What do you suppose it stands for?” I wondered.

“Could be the initials of the person supplying this crap.”

“If that’s the case, I’d say that means there’re two people supplying Power Suits in this city, the regular grey ones and this ‘DB’ variant.”

“Well, you know what that means.” Red sighed.

“What?”

“Two people trying to make money in the same marketplace, a bunch of other people buying up what is essentially a uniform supporting either supplier—in the criminal world, that’s a recipe for a gang war.”

Chapter 8

"**T**ake a look at this," said Chloe as she entered the APD's Recruitment Room, the same room I was in when I first arrived here. She flashed today's paper at me and read out the headline. "*Reporter Saved by Mystery Man Named 'Scar'.*"

I eyed the paper. A picture of me saving that woman from the mugger last night followed the headline. "Wow, what are the odds that someone would catch that on camera?"

Chloe stared at me curiously. "Given phone cameras are a thing, I'd say pretty fricking high."

"Oh, yeah. Right." Let's try not to make it so obvious that the last time I lived a normal, stable life in a house was back when phones still had numbered buttons on them.

"Anyway, I wouldn't be so happy about it, if I were you," she cautioned.

"About good publicity? Why not?"

"The APD is supposed to be a secret organization."

"Yeah, but we're not *that* kind of secret. I'm sure there are tons of conspiracy theorists out there who know about us. Same way they know about the division that deals with aliens. We just don't confirm our existence to anyone."

She nodded with feigned enthusiasm. "Uh-huh. And tell me, when's the last time you saw a member of the Extraterrestrial Department in the news?"

"I don't know. I mean, I'm sure it's happened at some point."

She shook her head. "Never. Not only did you manage to get yourself in the news, but you gave them your name, too. Director Agatha's going to be pissed."

"Quite the contrary, Ms. Chloe." Director Agatha had just entered with her hands behind her back. "Over the years, our exploits have become less and less secretive. We may not confirm our existence to them, but make no mistake, the public is starting to notice us. They're afraid, but I'd wager, with Mister Scar in the news, we can give the city hope while remaining secretive. I'd say that's the very definition of what we do here, not just keeping the public safe but making them feel safe as well."

"So you want him to be a vigilante?" asked Chloe.

The director shrugged. "Call him what you like—vigilante, hero, mascot."

"Yeah, 'cause I've always wanted to be a mascot," I grumbled.

"Steady on, Mister Scar. You should be honoured. Not many new recruits are promoted this quickly."

"Promoted, huh? Does that come with health benefits?"

She grinned at me and moved on. "I come bearing missions for the both of you. Ms. Chloe, I'm tasking you with an investigation. There have been reports of Mirror-Mind having been sighted in Sector Four. I'll need you to take a look."

"I'm on it," Chloe responded.

"You know how dangerous Kennedy is. Take Red with you."

"Will do." Chloe nodded and left the room briskly.

"As for you, Mister Scar, there are reports of a shadowy creature having been sighted in Sector Sixteen. The creature bears a striking resemblance to a woman who was kidnapped recently by the Adultnapper. She is highly hostile, and there have already been several casualties reported. I advise caution and haste, Mister Scar. Off you go."

At the director's command, I travelled to the Transport Room and teleported to Sector Sixteen.

***

When I arrived on the roof of a nearby building, I acquainted myself with Sector Sixteen, or as I knew it, Neetro City Square. It was a place that usually played host to various festivals and concerts. But this evening, it was hosting something very different. There were police cars surrounding the entire area, and in the centre of the square was a woman engulfed in some sort of shadowy haze.

I leaped from the rooftop and landed next to one of the police officers keeping a close vigil on the woman. He jumped and whipped his gun out, aiming it at me.

"Whoa, hey, same side," I said, throwing my hands in the air (not that I needed to; my suit would protect me if he decided to take the shot).

The officer took a breath. "Sorry. Just a little jumpy, I guess."

"I assume you have the situation handled, then," I smirked.

"Hardly," he sighed. "You're APD, right?"

"As advertised."

"I knew this shit was above my pay grade," he mumbled. Then he pointed a finger around the area. "Don't know if you've noticed, but all these things on the ground are bodies."

I looked where he was pointing. If I squinted, the "things" did resemble bodies, but they were shrivelled. They looked a little like ... like they were attacked by the *other* me. She couldn't ... could she? Does this woman have the same problem I have?

"We're at an impasse until this woman makes a move," the officer continued. "I don't want to provoke her, you know? She's killed enough people already."

"Any innocent people still in danger?" I asked.

"No. We evacuated everyone, closed off this whole area."

"Good. Can you point me toward whoever's in charge here?" I stared intensely at the motionless woman.

"Guess that'd be me. I'm the chief."

"Oh, even better. I want you to call off your officers. I'll take it from here."

The chief was shocked. "With all due respect, every officer here knew the risks of this job before taking it on. We're not going to just stand down for—"

"I don't care," I interrupted. "As an agent of the APD, I'm ordering you to fall back."

There was a short silence, fueled with tension. Then the chief activated his radio and spoke. "All officers, this is Chief Khan ordering you to fall back. I repeat: fall back."

In response, the police perimeter was swiftly broken as all the officers got in their cars and drove away to a safer distance.

The woman didn't react at all.

"I hope you know what you're doing," said the chief, turning toward his car.

"Yeah, I hope so, too," I muttered to myself.

The chief got in his car and drove away.

Now it was just me and the woman.

I walked—slowly. The woman didn't seem to notice me. She stared downward, her brown, tangled hair covering her eyes. Her skin was flowing with black veins.

She had olive-toned skin, but her veins were in such stark contrast to it, they almost made it look pale. She was dressed in something that was probably really nice once, but now it was torn, stained, and unwoven at the shoulders. Her entire body was shrouded in this dark, shadowy mist. Fitting for such a mysterious woman.

What happened to her? She's supposedly one of the recently kidnapped victims, or at least, she *looks* like one of the victims. But there's something off, something not entirely human. She looks like me ... when I'm *not* me. The black veins, the monstrous persona—all she's missing is my scar. I barely remember how I got my scar, but however it happened, what if that wasn't the end of it? Are there others like me? Is she like me? Maybe it's a disease, something you can catch, quick, random. Or maybe ... maybe someone's doing this to people ... on purpose. She was kidnapped. Who knows what happened to her during that time?

I stopped walking, and the woman looked up at me. Now I was closer, the mist was a little easier to see through, and I could see that her face was scratched and bruised. There may have been no sign of a glowing red scar there, but her eyes were piercing red.

Then I froze, in thought and motion. Alerted by my sixth sense, I noticed a twitch in the woman's stance. She was about to attack.

She sprung into the air, and the dark mist rushed to her hands, forming shadowy, demonic claws that fit her like gloves. Sidestepping out of the way, I avoided her attack, but that didn't stop her. She was relentless, and her attacks were continuous. She hissed like an animal fighting for survival. Her claw swipes were fast and strong. Even with my enhanced abilities, it was difficult to avoid her assault. So difficult, in fact, that one of her attacks actually connected, followed by another, and another. Before I knew it, I was on the ground with the woman crouching over me. She looked at me like I was the first meal she'd seen in years, and knowing how my scar works, that's probably exactly how she saw me.

I needed an exit before she literally sucked the life out of me. I activated my Claws and swiped at her face before she could continue her attack. She backed off and pressed her hands to her face—they weren't demonic claws anymore. Blood seeped through her fingers, but it wasn't red, it was black. And it smelled strange, like ... burning coal?

She stared at me, seething, as I slowly returned to my feet. For a few seconds, we stared at each other, her red eyes glaring at me between the black blood dripping from her face. But then her skin blackened, and she was gone. She sunk into a shadow as if it were water. I couldn't see her anymore, but my sixth sense told me she was still here. Just because I could sense her, though, didn't mean I had an advantage. I was still knocked to the ground when she popped out of the shadows, lunged at me, and then dove into the shadows again. Sure, I could sense her coming, but in the shadows, she was significantly faster—and I could barely keep up with her before. I couldn't react in time. If only I could see her in the shadows … Wait, maybe I can.

The idea was ready; I just had to put it into play. I activated my Visor and switched it to Thermal, and just as I'd thought, I could see her heat signature in the shadows. The colour was pretty red; she ran hotter than most people, like she had a fever.

Now that I could see her, I could react to her red figure swimming through the shadows. I blocked her attacks and threw punches when she was vulnerable, and in no time, she fell to the ground, exhausted and beaten.

Deactivating my Visor, I stared at her. She was heaving, clutching her stomach. She reminded me of a wounded, starving cat. She doubled over and vomited something yellow and black, and the smell of burning coal returned, but it was more acidic this time. Then she fell unconscious and collapsed into her own puke. Only by her moving chest did I know she was still alive. Otherwise, it looked like she had just dropped dead right there. I couldn't help thinking of myself as I stared at her. When I'm not myself, when I'm like her … I eat people—suck out their life. If I didn't, though, if I could stop myself or someone else could stop me, would I end up like her? Starving? Vomiting? … What happened to her?

You know, there is one difference between her and me. When I'm not myself, it's like I'm a completely different person, but she seems so lifeless, almost like a puppet.

A police car drove up toward me and stopped. From it emerged the police chief I'd spoken to before.

"Well, I must say, I'm glad you came," he said. "Evacuating and blocking off the area was all I had in the idea department." He chuckled darkly.

I didn't respond. I was too concerned with who this woman was and how she got like this. Plus, the adrenaline was wearing off, and I was beginning to realize just how badly my ass got kicked.

"You all right?" the chief asked.

"Huh? Oh, yeah, I'm fine." I spawned a pair of handcuffs from my suit and attached them to the woman's wrists. "These are special handcuffs for people with enhanced strength," I explained. "But be careful. Remember, she's not dead. She could start attacking again at any moment. The cuffs can sedate her if she tries to break free, but I wouldn't put all your faith in that. I'll follow you back to the station, just in case anything happens. There, you're going to have her transferred to APD forensics. Hopefully, they can figure out how she got like this."

The chief nodded solemnly.

We got in the police car, seating the woman in the back, and drove to the police station. I oversaw things there until the forensic scientists from the APD arrived to take the woman away. This situation must have really hit me hard. I was acting like … like an APD agent, like none of this fazed me.

I left after the woman was transferred, ducking into an alleyway and contacting the Transporter to take me back to the APD headquarters.

***

"This is reporter Jazmine Humble live at the scene of what was quite a horrific event," said the woman on the monitor in the APD's Recruitment Room. "Witnesses report that earlier today a woman shrouded in shadow violently attacked several people at Neetro City Square. It seems that the woman was trying to extract some sort of energy from her victims. A witness described this energy as, quote, 'something akin to life force found in fantasy stories.' The energy in question was allegedly yellow in colour, and the woman seemed to feed on it. Forty people have been confirmed dead as a result of her rampage.

"The woman was stopped by a returning character going by the name of *Scar*, whom you may remember from an earlier story we covered when he saved reporter Ellen Chen from a robbery. The shadow-shrouded woman is currently in police custody. We've reached out to the Neetro City Police Department, but they have refused to comment on the situation. As you can see behind me, there has been no serious damage done to the area, and Neetro City Square should reopen to the public soon. This is reporter Jazmine Humble for Neetro City News. Now to Aoife Price for the weather report."

"Look at you in the spotlight," Chloe remarked as she turned her focus away from the news report.

"Yep, I'm a walking mascot. Exactly what I signed up for." I rolled my eyes.

"Mascot or not, I'd say you did a pretty good job handling that. Thinking to use the Thermal mode on your Visor to track the woman when she disappeared was genius. You're getting better at this job, rookie."

I wanted to smile at the compliment, but I couldn't. This was going to haunt me for a while. How did that woman get like that?

"Scar, you okay?" Chloe asked.

"Uh, yeah ... yeah, um, do you ... do you know if forensics found out anything about that woman?"

"Yeah, she died."

"What?"

"Her DNA was only half human. They're still trying to figure out what the other half was, but it was poisoning her. Her heart stopped when they drew her blood."

... She died.

What does that mean for me?

"So how did your mission go? Did you find Mirror-Mind?" I said, changing the subject to something that wouldn't add to my anxiety.

"Unfortunately, we missed him, but we did find this." Chloe pressed her hand to the wall beside the monitor, and a picture replaced the news feed.

The picture showed a man sprawled on the ground. He was beyond recognition due to the plentiful gashes on his face. Above him, written on a wall in what I assumed was blood, was the word *ticktock*.

"Who did this?" I asked.

"Guess."

"Mirror-Mind?"

"Exactly," Red butted in as he entered the room. "Only, one thing is out of place. Kennedy has always been known as a random, anarchical killer. Yet now he's killing people and using their blood to write time-related words: *ticktock, time, wristwatch,* etc. His obsession with time has been a thing for a while now, but it seems to be getting worse. It's almost like he believes he's running out of time."

"What, no *hello*, just straight to the point?" I said.

"We don't have time for that. Kennedy was just spotted in Sector Eleven. You and I are going to go get him."

"Whoa, what the hell!" Chloe objected. "You're taking him and not me? I'm the one who helped you get all this information."

"Not my decision. Director Agatha has something else for you, something about interrogating prisoners about their Power Suits."

"Oh, come on, not an interrogation," Chloe groaned. "I hate doing that. Especially with prisoners; they're always such dicks."

"Well, best not keep them waiting. I hear they can get deflated if you wait too long," I joked.

She looked at me. "What was that, a dick joke?"

"What, you didn't like it?"

"Meh, not your best."

I shrugged. "Hey, they can't all be wieners."

Red chuckled gruffly.

"Really?" said Chloe. "The dad joke made you chuckle. All right, I'm done. I hate all of you." She marched off.

"So, you're a dad joke kind of guy," I said to Red.

"You and I need to get going as well." Red ignored me and walked off.

"Yes, sir," I said, mocking his straightforward attitude.

I sighed and followed him to the Transport Room.

Chapter 9

"So, Red," I called out to my reclusive ally as we ran across the rooftops in the dead of night, in search of Mirror-Mind.

"We're focusing on the mission," he commanded.

"We can do that and talk at the same time."

There was no response.

"Come on, Red. Mr. Rouge."

"Don't call me that."

"Okay, just Red, then. I notice I don't know much about you."

"That's no accident."

"Well, tell me something about yourself."

Silence.

"Come on, anything."

My rooftop running was suddenly halted by Red's outstretched arm as he directed my attention to the event taking place in an empty parking lot below. A group of about twenty people were entering the area, armed with baseball bats, rifles, and Power Suits—the brown kind.

They also appeared to be wearing dog masks. Don't ask why.

"What do you think's going on here?" I asked Red.

"My guess is this is the start of that gang war I knew would happen eventually. We'd better stay here and watch over this."

"What about Mirror-Mind?"

Red rubbed the stress out of his eyes with two fingers. "This is going to make matters more difficult. Uh … you stay here and watch over this. I'll continue looking for Kennedy. Keep in touch if you need me."

"Roger that," I said.

Red leaped over to the next rooftop and continued his search. I jumped down to confront this gang. (Probably best I intervene before things get too ugly.)

They seemed surprised by my sudden appearance, but they didn't attack me. Not yet anyway.

"What's with the dog masks, guys, are you in a band?" I said. They all just stared at me blankly. "Oh, okay, I get it. You're all just trying to do me the courtesy of protecting my innocent eyes from the ugly faces your mothers gave you."

One man approached me, clearly trying to restrain his anger as he removed his dog mask and rubbed the tension from his face. He spoke very quietly, pointing a finger at me. "You talking shit about my mother?"

"What? No, not your mother, your face."

A look of confusion graced the expressions of my entire audience.

I sighed. "Never mind. Good jokes are so wasted on people like you anyway." I shook my head disappointedly.

"Man, can I blow this guy's head off now?" someone called out.

"Save your ammo," said the guy in front of me. "It's not him we're after."

"I don't suppose you'd want to tell me who it is you're after, would you?" I asked.

He pointed behind me. "Them."

I turned and saw another group of twenty or so people also armed with baseball bats, rifles, and Power Suits—the grey kind. I was right in the middle of what looked like the start of quite the epic fight between rival gangs.

"Well, would you look at that," said someone with a grey Power Suit. "Someone let the puppies out to play. Where's your boss?"

"Busy," answered someone in a dog mask. "She ain't got time for your guys' bullshit."

"You mean she ain't got time to watch us wipe the floor with the puppy pack?" Several members of the grey-Power-Suit gang laughed.

"Puppy pack, huh?" I said to the grey-Power-Suit gang. "So who are you guys, then, the kitty crusaders?"

I got a few chuckles from the dog-mask gang.

"I'm sorry, who the hell are you?" said someone with a grey Power Suit.

"Oh, you know," I shrugged, "I'm just some guy who'd prefer not to have a shoot-out happen in his neighbourhood."

"If you're smart, you'll stay out of this. This doesn't concern you."

"You're probably right," I agreed. "But my IQ's not that high, so ..."

And with that, the battle began.

My first priority was disabling the rifles. I didn't want this to get too ugly too fast. Using my Tractor Palm, I pulled all the guns to me and emptied the bullets onto the ground. Simple. Actually, this whole fight was simple, given the advantage my nanobot suit gave me. It was definitely far superior to the suits that these gangs were wearing. (That's why you should never buy a knockoff.) But then my sixth sense called my attention. Not to a danger in this battle, but to a danger that was just metres away ... I ducked as a bullet soared through the air and pierced through three heads before stopping. So much for not wanting this to get ugly; now there's blood and brains all over the ground.

My head darted in the direction the bullet came from. There, standing atop a dumpster just barely within the parking lot's perimeter, I saw him—stained white vest, blond hair, and that insane look in his eyes. The shot came from Mirror-Mind, though he didn't have a gun on him.

"Headshot!" he yelled. "Let's see if I can do any better."

Mirror-Mind held out his fist, and a bullet hole emerged from the top of his wrist. With the guidance of my senses, I pushed the endangered gang members out of the way before they were hit by the next shot. The bullet ended up hitting a wall a little ways away, crumbling some of the brick.

"What's the matter with you? What are you doing?" I yelled at him.

"Oh, don't mind me. I'm just testing some things out." Mirror-Mind readied his fist and grinned. "Third time's the charm."

Before he could fire, he was knocked to the ground courtesy of a well-placed kick from Red, who had just caught up with him.

"Well, that hurt," Mirror-Mind laughed.

Luckily, I didn't need to keep all my attention on the battle at hand; my sixth sense was doing most of the work. I chose to partially focus on the battle between Red and Mirror-Mind.

"Here's how this is going to work," said Red. "You're going to surrender yourself. I will handcuff you and take you in, and you'll be quiet about it."

Mirror-Mind stumbled to his feet. "And why would I do that?"

"Because I'm not giving you a choice." Red pulled Mirror-Mind toward him, arm first, through the use of his Tractor Palm. "I figured when you started shooting bullets out of your arm, that meant there was some kind of metal inside you. Looks like I was right."

But then, a wave of electricity discharged from Mirror-Mind's arm and shocked Red's hand off of him. "Is it better to be right, or is it better to be smart?"

Mirror-Mind glanced at me. "Need a hand?"

I moved out of the way of someone's fist, letting it knock out the guy behind me. "I'm good. Any help you're planning on giving will probably be a lot bloodier than I'd like. If you want to stick around and wait, though, that'd be great."

He grinned. "You'll need my help eventually, and I plan to give it to you, but I need to find the source of the infection first. That's what he told me. Of course, that won't matter if I don't get this stupid watch fixed." He examined his wristwatch carefully. "Complicated piece of technology, this is. I don't even remember where I got it from; it's so old. Though ... I don't remember him having one ..."

He stopped then, like his thoughts were loading. Red was slowly recovering from the attack, and I was almost done dealing with this gang fight.

Mirror-Mind scratched his head, grasping his hair between his fingers. "Why can't I remember? I knew this before, or I will, but I can't even remember how I forgot."

"I don't know what the hell you're talking about," said Red, now fully recovered, "but I've had enough of your games, Kennedy."

He looked at Red sharply. "You think this is a game? Do you think I do what I do because it's fun? If you knew the things I know, the things I should know … maybe then you'd understand. Time is always ticking; she is always watching."

"You can tell me all about your obsession with time when I take you in." Red approached Mirror-Mind.

"I wouldn't come any closer if I were you. The shock I gave you before was mild compared to what I can do. I don't want to have to kill you."

Red stopped. "Since when have you cared about not killing people?"

"Since you became important to him." He pointed at me. "I may be testing things out, but that's something I don't need to test. I don't want to interfere more than I have to." He grinned. "Anyway, time's ticking." Then he faded and disappeared.

At the same time, I'd finished with these gangs. Everyone who came here to fight today ended up unconscious.

"You know, I always wonder how Mirror-Mind does that vanishing trick," I said.

"Probably the same way he can shoot bullets from his arm." Red sighed and cursed under his breath. "Mirror-Mind's smarter than he seems. His bodily enhancements are part of what makes him so difficult to capture."

"Speaking of capture, what are we going to do with all these unconscious gangsters lying about?"

"I'll inform Director Agatha. She can send some field agents in to clean up here. I'll meet you back at HQ." Red contacted the Transporter and was quickly teleported away.

I sighed. "He's really not much of a talker."

I was about to follow Red's lead when I heard a voice calling me in a hushed tone. "Hey, Mr. Big Shot Hero."

The voice came from a man in a brown trench coat and fedora standing at the edge of the parking lot. "Come over here," he whispered. "I've got something for you."

I approached the man. "What is this, the forties? I hate to break it to you, but I don't think a trench coat and fedora is considered an inconspicuous outfit anymore."

He smiled at me, stifling a laugh. "That's good. She said you were funny."

"Who's she?"

The man pulled a white card from his coat pocket. "She wants to see you."

"All right, I'll bite. Give me this tip of yours or whatever it is."

I took the card. It was just an address, and it was signed "DB".

When I looked up from the card, the man was already on his way. Before he was out of earshot, though, he said, "That's courtesy of the Dog Burglar. She said you'd know what that meant."

Chapter 10

"So you believe that this Dog Burglar, who's given you this invitation, is actually your friend?" asked Director Agatha as we walked down the corridors of the APD's headquarters.

"Right." I nodded. "Her name is Christine Summers. Before I joined the APD, Christine and I were small-time crooks. We were homeless and only stole what we needed. We were all each other had ... I'm afraid something bad might've happened to her after I left."

"What makes you so certain that the Dog Burglar and Christine Summers are one and the same?" Director Agatha looked at the Dog Burglar's invitation, holding the white card in her hands.

"Well, for one thing," I pointed at the invitation, "that's her handwriting. And secondly, the name *Dog Burglar* isn't new. That's a bit of a nickname she's had for a while."

We stopped at our destination—the Transport Room.

"Maybe I should send someone else for this task," the director said.

"No!" Whoa, little loud. Calm down. "Sorry, I mean ... Christine ... she can be difficult. She doesn't trust people very easily. I know how to talk to her."

The director sighed and handed me the invitation. "Be careful, Mister Scar. Don't let your emotions get in the way. Whoever this Dog Burglar is, they're dangerous, and they control a good percentage of the crime in this city. The Dog Burglar must be stopped."

"I understand."

"By any means necessary, Mister Scar." I was silent as she fixed me with an accusatory stare.

"I'll be sending you reinforcements," she continued, "just in case you need help."

"I won't need help."

"But you will get it all the same. Don't worry, you'll still get first crack at the Dog Burglar, but you won't be alone." Director Agatha placed her hand on my shoulder. "Good luck, Mister Scar."

She continued down the corridor, and I entered the Transport Room.

I looked at the invitation in my hands. It was signed "DB" in Christine's handwriting. There's no doubt it's her ... I just hope she's not doing something stupid. Sometimes Christine needs someone to hold her back; she can't control herself. She lets her fear and anxiety drive her desire to control everything around her, at her own expense. I just hope she's okay ... I hope it wasn't a mistake to not try to reach out to her sooner.

I read out the address to the central device in the room. "Calculating," said the robotic voice. "Sending Agent Scar to Sector Three. Are you ready to proceed?"

"Affirmative," I sighed.

***

From the rooftops, I peered down at my destination. It was just an unassuming building backdropped by the dark, gloomy dawn, like any other building in this city. It looked like an abandoned apartment complex maybe. I activated my Visor and switched it to X-ray mode. Through the lenses, I saw that the interior of the building was crawling with guards. They were unarmed, but they were wearing brown Power Suits with the "DB" initials on them.

I deactivated the Visor and spotted two more guards standing outside near the entrance of the building. Both were wearing dog masks.

"Okay," I thought out loud. "How should I do this? I want to get a good look at this place while I'm here. You never know, I may find some information about how these Power Suits work, or who's supplying the grey ones. I doubt Christine made the brown ones; she's not that way inclined. I guess I should start at the bottom of the building and work my way through. I'll have a lot of guards to deal with, but that shouldn't be a problem." I looked at the white card in my hand. "After all, I was invited."

I leaped off the roof and made my way to the front entrance. The two guards stood at the door, unmoving.

"Turn around," one guard said. "You don't belong here."

"Actually," I showed them the card, "I've been invited."

If you're thinking that they then escorted me to their boss nicely and without issue, you have too much faith in the people of this city. They responded with their fists. I stored the invitation within my suit and made quick work of them, laying their unconscious bodies up against the wall.

"Wow, guys, great people skills. I feel really invited," I joked.

Opening the derelict, wooden door, I entered the building. Surprisingly, I wasn't met with any more opposition ... not yet at least. The interior of the building was filled with hallways, staircases, and rooms. This was definitely some sort of apartment building or crappy hotel before. The paint was peeling off the walls, and there were stains everywhere ... and a fair amount of those stains were red.

I took a breath and continued through the various hallways and up the various staircases, checking every room I could find. A lot of those rooms were empty, but some had stacks of money and others had boxes of circuitry and fabrics. Eventually, all my snooping did find me some resistance in the form of more people in dog masks. I handled them without issue, but I was really starting to think my invitation was delivered by mistake.

When I got to the top floor, there was only one room— no door, just a small entryway with a floor mat. The mat had a picture of a menacing cartoon bulldog sewn into it. Fitting entrance for the "Dog Burglar." I guess this is the place. I entered.

The room was big, about twice the size of an average living room. A large, rectangular table with a TV screen for a top acted as the room's centrepiece. Chairs surrounded the table, and the whole room was shrouded in low light coming from a large window.

"Well, took you long enough," said a woman emerging from a dark corner of the room. She wore a slightly modified Power Suit. It was still brown with yellow streaks, and it still had "DB" inscribed on the chest, but there were also hints of black that added sleekness to the design. The woman adjusted her black, fingerless gloves as she steadily approached.

It was her. Christine. She looked no different from when I'd seen her last. Curly, ginger hair, brown eyes, and olive-toned cheeks that were covered in freckles.

She ran to me and threw her arms around my neck. For a moment, everything felt right again. Everything felt like it could go back to how it was ... only for a moment.

"Oh, my god, Scar, I missed you," she whispered.

"I missed you, too."

I held her close, prolonging this happy moment. I didn't need my sixth sense to know that the conversation I would have to have with her was not going to be a fun one ... if it would even be a conversation, that is.

She let me go and stared into my eyes for a second. I got the feeling she was really looking at my scar, though. I always liked to forget it even existed, but she always liked to wonder when the next time would be ... if it ever *wouldn't* be.

A ringing sound accompanied by a telephone icon appearing on the table monitor pulled Christine away from me. "Sorry," she said as she rushed over to the table and tapped on the icon with her finger. A man in a dog mask appeared on the screen.

"What?" Christine scowled with her arms crossed.

"Boss," the man answered, "looks like Lincoln's upped his security. We're at one of his warehouses, but it looks like he's had some insane locks installed."

"I don't doubt it. That bastard's probably tired of us stealing his stuff." She smiled.

"I think we're going to need more time to get into this place, boss."

"You don't have more time. Lincoln's dirty cops will get there soon, and they'll be very eager to use their arresting you to kiss his ass. If you take too long, you'll have to fight them off."

"Then, uh, do we have your permission to abort?"

"Your suit works, right?"

"Uh, yeah."

"Then I don't want to hear any more bullshit out of you. Grow some balls, handle anyone that gets in your way, and get the parts I told you to get."

"But, boss—"

"Do you remember what happens to puppies who don't follow the pack?"

There was a change in the man after Christine said that. He suddenly seemed calmer, like when you're so scared shitless that you just give up and let whatever happens happen.

"Right. Sorry, boss," he said. "I'll handle it."

"Good. Don't disappoint me." Christine tapped the screen, disconnecting the call.

Christine was different ... at least, I wanted to think she was, but this was just the worst side of her coming out. Her controlling, commanding nature, her defence mechanisms in overdrive. This is how she protects herself when she's afraid.

"Sorry about that," she said to me lightly.

I looked at her. "So, the famous Dog Burglar stands before me." I had to address the elephant in the room at some point.

She shrugged. "Having a motif helps to keep everyone in line."

"I bet it does." I scratched the back of my head. "I thought you only stole what you needed to survive. Isn't that one of your rules?"

"It is, and that's what I'm doing."

"You really think you need to be a crime boss to survive? I mean, come on, Christine, you're running a good percentage of the crime in this city. I think that counts as a luxury."

"Forty-two percent, actually." She smiled.

"What?"

"I run forty-two percent of crime in this city."

"And you're proud of that?"

"Hell yeah, I am. I went from living on the streets to stumbling upon a warehouse shipment of the prototypes for the Power Suits. I spent a bit of time following the trucks and keeping track of the shipping routes until I had a few good guesses as to who was making them. All it took was for me to steal his designs for the suits and establish myself as a competitor. I changed the suits' colour scheme and a few other things, but they're essentially the same as the original design. And just like that, I'm making his profits my profits."

"Who's *he*?"

Christine grinned. "That's the part you're not going to believe. Thomas Lincoln."

"The billionaire?"

"The billionaire." She nodded.

Thomas Lincoln was one of those guys who was famous for being rich. He didn't make his fortune by founding a huge tech company or being an incredible actor. I always assumed he got his money through inheritance or being really good with stocks or something else just as boring, but maybe there was a lot more criminal activity involved than I thought. Well, I guess that answers one question.

"He makes a lot of his money by selling his suits to people," Christine continued. "I'm the bitch who keeps cutting into his margins ... his words, not mine. I could take over his whole operation so easily."

"I don't doubt it," I agreed.

"But I won't. As long as he's running more crime than me, he'll be taking most of the heat from the authorities. He's got a lot of cops in his pocket, but he doesn't know where I am. As long as it stays that way, I'm free to do what I want."

"And what do you want?"

"You ... I want you by my side again." She stepped closer to me. "What happened to you? I saw on the news you're some kind of vigilante now?"

"Yeah, I, uh ... I got mixed up with some weird people." I didn't want to say too much. The existence of the APD is supposed to be a secret, even from Christine.

"Well, that made you easier to track down so I could send you the invitation. Which reminds me." She walked back to the table. "I didn't just invite you here because I missed you." She ushered me over with a wave of her hand. I joined her at the table, and she double tapped the screen. A keypad appeared, and she entered a password hidden behind black dots. When she finished, the keypad disappeared, and a video feed took its place. It depicted a ginger-haired woman in an empty room. She was tied to a chair and looked like she'd been beaten half to death.

"Who is that?" I asked.

"My mom."

I stared at Christine, shocked.

"I know. A couple of my guys are good at tracking people down, so I got them to track her down for me. Couldn't find my dad, though. That asshole's long gone."

I stared at the woman on the screen; she was covered in bruises and blood.

"What happened to her?" I asked.

Christine grew a sinister smile. "I did. She ignored me for years, content to just drink herself to sleep. But when I was a teenager, then she was interested in me. Everything was accidental at first—she just happened to nudge my chest, or she didn't realize her hand was just a little too comfortable in my lap. But then it was all, 'You came out of me, so everything about you belongs to me.' She was just making sure her 'possession' was developing nicely." She winced at her own words. "No wonder Dad left her. Got away while he could, even if he didn't want to take me."

This was my fault. I knew this about Christine's mother; I knew this about Christine. This was the worst side of her, and I knew it could come out. I left her, and I thought for a second that she'd be better off if I didn't try to find her ... and look what happened.

"This is wrong, Christine," I said.

She glared at me. "What the hell are you talking about? She deserves this."

"But you're becoming someone you're not. You're using your power to control, manipulate, and abuse the people around you."

"You don't understand. I'm not defenceless anymore. I'm not a bottom feeder on the streets anymore. I have assets, resources. I'm finally on top; *we're* finally on top." She was begging me to agree with her, but I couldn't. Her face fell. "How are you going to just stand there and judge me? You left. I didn't know if they threw you in jail, or if you got killed. Then, next thing I know, you're in the news with a whole new life, like you forgot all about me."

"I didn't forget anything. I just … I'm in a complicated situation, and I thought … I thought it'd be better if I left you out of it. But I was wrong, Christine, and you need to listen to me, you have to stop this. This isn't you." I glanced at the video feed of her mother. "I can't let you hurt anyone."

She followed my eyes to the table screen. "So I'm supposed to just let her get away with it?"

"Of course not, but this isn't you, Christine, it's her. The control, the fear tactics, it's everything she instilled in you. Isn't that what you explained to me that time I called you a control freak?"

She bit her lip. "Wow. You'd think the one person who knows me best would understand."

"I do understand—"

"Do you! Why can't you see what I'm building here? For us. We don't have to live on the streets anymore, we don't have to struggle anymore; when people step all over us, we can step on them even harder." She pointed to her mother on the screen as she squirmed in the chair she was bound to. "She deserves everything I have coming to her. She put me where I was, and I clawed myself up to where I am."

I just shook my head. I never should have left her.

Her eyes were watering, and she was smiling like she couldn't believe my reaction to all this. "I don't ... I just, I thought you'd ..." She wiped her eyes. "Why did you even come here?"

"I'm worried about you."

"Don't be. I'm fine. And so are you, apparently. I see you on the news all the time, fighting all these crazy criminals ..." Then she smiled contentedly. "That's it, isn't it? I'm just some criminal for you to stop. That's why you're really here."

"I want to help you."

There was a shiver down my spine, but I couldn't avoid what was coming. One jab from Christine's fist was enough to push me back a few feet. But it didn't stop there. She continued to attack, and she was so fast that my sixth sense was practically useless. I didn't know if her Power Suit was better than the ones I'd encountered before or if she was just a better fighter than the people I usually meet. She was angry, though. She flung her fists at me like an enraged boxer, and she was winning this fight.

I caught her fist and tried to restrain her, but she just rammed me with her shoulder and knocked me to the floor. It was only thanks to a beeping sound coming from the table that she stopped whaling on me. I could taste blood in my mouth, and I could see droplets of it on the floor.

"Shit," Christine breathed, staring at the table screen. The sound of police sirens was blaring from outside. "How did they find this place?"

She looked at me and grimaced as if she suspected I had something to do with the cops coming here. I suppose I might have done. Maybe these were Director Agatha's reinforcements.

Christine retrieved a baseball bat from underneath the table, and for a second, I was afraid she was going to beat me with it, but she went over to the window instead and swung it through the glass. The sirens blared much louder now.

I struggled without success to pick myself up off the floor. "Christine, wait," I said weakly.

She didn't even look at me. She just leaped out of the window with the bat in hand.

I had to follow her. With her Power Suit, she definitely would have survived that fall, and I knew she'd be able to avoid the police. But I was too weak. My suit would heal me eventually, but it couldn't do it fast enough for me to catch up to her.

I lost her.

The police arrived through the entryway, scoping out the area and confirming that there were no immediate threats. With them was a woman with straight black hair and a black, skin-tight suit. Chloe.

"You all right?" she asked me, lending me her hand and helping me to my feet.

"Fine, yeah. Thanks," I responded absently. "Um, there's a woman somewhere in this building. She's tied to a chair and—"

"I know. We found her before we found you."

"Okay, good. She's not necessarily innocent, though. She's Christine's mother; she abused her."

"Well, she'll be judged by a higher power now. She's dead."

I stared at Chloe. "What? What do you mean she's dead?"

"Well I'm not a detective, or a forensic scientist, or anything like that, but it looked to me like she found a way to free herself from her bonds, and then she bashed her head into the wall. We found her on the floor with severe head trauma, to put it lightly."

I looked down and breathed shallowly. "I'm not sure how to feel about that."

Chloe stared at me. "Are you sure you're all right? 'Cause you look pretty bad."

I smiled. "My suit heals me, right? I'll be fine."

I would be fine, but I'm afraid Christine won't be.

***

About an hour later, I was in the APD's Recruitment Room. I was almost fully healed of my physical wounds, but my emotional ones lingered. Chloe stood, arms crossed, watching the news on the monitor.

"We are live, just outside the alleged hideout of the dreaded Dog Burglar, a recent addition to the city's insidious group of underworld crime bosses," the reporter said. "Witnesses claim that some sort of battle took place within the previously believed abandoned apartment building, but it appears the Dog Burglar escaped through the top floor window and is likely still at large. It is believed by police that her operation has taken a big hit today, and she will be looking for an opportunity to rebuild her reputation and her following. We here at Neetro City News implore everyone to stay safe and keep away from anyone wearing a Power Suit. If you think you've seen the Dog Burglar, police ask that you keep your distance and contact the Neetro City Police Department immediately."

In the background, I could make out some police officers escorting a screaming man into a police car. Though faint, his words could be heard on the news report: "I ain't saying nothing! She'll kill me if I do! I'm no rat!"

The reporter continued. "Um … yes, well, with that, I'm Jazmine Humble with Neetro City News. Connor, back to you."

The scene changed to an indoor setting, and another reporter spoke. "Thank you, Jazmine. Despite the yelling we were able to hear in the background there, not all of the Dog Burglar's followers are so loyal. One has informed the police that the Dog Burglar's true identity is Christine Summers, whom you may recall was the subject of a missing person case several years ago." A picture of Christine was shown. It was from before she ran away from home; she must have been sixteen in it. "Mirroring my fellow reporter's words, if anyone has information on the whereabouts of this woman, you are urged to call the police immediately. Keep in mind, this is an old image, and Ms. Summers is currently around twenty-five years of age."

The reporter continued by speaking about the two types of Power Suits and how the public could recognize them.

"Scar, I'm sorry about your friend," said Chloe as she turned down the volume of the news report with her finger pressed to the side of the monitor. "This must all be a big shock to you."

"That's just it," I said. "It isn't. This is something I knew she was capable of … if she were pushed." I sighed. "I don't know what I'm going to do."

"We'll find her."

"How do you figure? She could be anywhere by now."

"We'll find her because it's our job to get dangerous criminals off the street. And she's not too dangerous to contain; she doesn't need to be assassinated. We just need to take that suit off of her, and then she's just a woman who needs help. We can give her that."

I nodded, chuckling to relieve a bit of the tension within me. "This has to be the weirdest thing that's ever happened to me."

"You want a bet?" Chloe challenged.

"Why? You've got something weirder?"

"Listen to this: Remember that shadow woman you fought?"

"The one that looked like one of the kidnapping victims?"

"That's the one." She nodded. "Turns out, she wasn't kidnapped at all. The reason she looked like one of the kidnapped people is because she was the biological daughter of one of them."

"Okay," I said, trying to wrap my head around this.

"It gets better. Her mother, the one who's still missing, never had a daughter, only a son. This shadow woman never even existed, meaning she must have been born while the mother was missing."

"But that doesn't make any sense," I objected. "The kidnappings only started a little while ago. That woman was at least twenty when I saw her."

"Exactly. She was a woman with half-human, half-unknown DNA who has no birth record—no identity of any kind—and was born, grew to maturity, and poisoned to death by her own DNA, all within the year."

Well that's a big difference between me and her. Aside from my ten-year hibernation, I'm pretty sure I lived through all twenty-four years of my life in real-time. "Okay, you win," I said. "That is weird."

"Told you. Oh, I almost forgot. I'm sending an address to your suit."

"An address?"

"The location of your next mission. Director Agatha told me to give it to you. You said your friend said she stole the Power Suit designs from Thomas Lincoln, right? That's the address of his main office, which is also the address closest to the meeting place where a lot of people are getting these Power Suits from. That's according to the intel I got from the prisoners I interrogated yesterday. The director wants you to pay Lincoln a visit."

"Ugh, a rich businessman crime boss?" I complained. "Can I take a sick day instead?"

"We don't get sick days."

"Of course we don't," I sighed. "I'm telling you, a human resources department would work wonders for morale here."

"Yeah, I'm sure it would," she chuckled.
I started off on my way to the Transport Room.
"Have fun," Chloe called behind me.
"Totally won't," I drawled.

Chapter 11

In my line of work, you start to realize that every criminal with money and power follows a very specific trend: They all reside at the top of tall buildings. Whether that's a symbolic thing or just coincidental is beside the point; as the person who has to stop criminals from doing what they do, I always end up having to climb up the huge building. So, why am I using my Claws to scale a, give or take, fifty-storey building? Well, instead of using the elevator like the lazy-ass person I'd like to be, I have to climb the outside wall of this building because—and this is the good part—the elevator doesn't actually go to the top floor, which is where I need to be. And yes, I checked before I started climbing. One thing's for sure, when I get to the top of this thing, Thomas Lincoln is totally getting a piece of my mind.

Furious rant aside, I have a target, and after a long climb, I'm finally looking right at him. Well, I'm looking at him from outside a window while shivering from the high-altitude winds, but same difference.

Thomas Lincoln himself was huge. The amount of muscle he had made him look like a mountain wrapped in a grey tuxedo. He sat at a brown, wooden desk in the centre of the room, atop a red, circular rug on a carpeted, blue floor. To the left, there were bookshelves, and to the right, a leather couch. How quaint.

I pressed my hand to the window and easily slid it open. It wasn't even locked. Guess that makes life easier for me. I entered and sat on the windowsill. "Sorry for the intrusion," I said. "It was freezing out there. Windy, too. Thomas Lincoln, I presume?"

He looked at me, not at all fazed by my sudden appearance. With a deep voice, he answered. "Indeed."

"Not very smart, you know, leaving your window open. That's how burglars get in."

Slowly, he stood from his desk. "Being on the top floor, one does not expect intrusion from such an obscure location."

"Well then, here's a thought, maybe you should get an elevator that goes all the way to the top floor. You know, in case someone wants to pay you a visit." I grinned.

He nodded calmly. "Apologies, I didn't catch your name."

"I didn't give it."

"You're not working for that bitch, are you?"

"Why? Are you expecting someone from Union?"

He sighed. "If you're not part of that bitch's pack of puppies, then why are you here?"

"Oh, sorry, I thought that was obvious. Here, I'll make it simple. You, bad guy. Me, good guy. Good guy stop bad guy doing bad things. Are you following me here?"

Lincoln's serious face stretched into a smile. "I do believe I recall seeing you pictured in the newspaper. A vigilante. At best, you're a hero, at worst, you're a nuisance. I'm curious, what makes you think I'm such a bad man?"

"Well, the main thing is the manufacturing and distribution of Power Suits, as well as profiting off those affairs. I'm sure there're other things, too, but I'm focused on the Power Suits mostly. Oh, and also, we can't ignore the fact that I broke in here, and you instantly thought I was working for the Dog Burglar. Talk about being tangled up in crime."

"So you've heard of her?" He crossed his arms.

"So have you, or else you wouldn't be expecting an assassination attempt from her."

"I'm a very rich man, and the Dog Burglar is a criminal who is still at large according to the news. I expect every lawbreaker to target me. It's an occupational hazard."

"I'll bet it is. Like I said, though, I'm just a good guy, sitting in front of a bad guy, asking him to cut the crap and give himself up."

Lincoln stepped away from his desk and stood about two metres from me. "You seem very adamant that I am a bad guy, but do you have any proof?"

"Proof?"

"Well, a vigilante like yourself can't barge in here with the intention of stopping a situation you deem as criminal without proof."

"Funny, you seem very adamant that I'm a vigilante. Think that's called the pot calling the kettle black."

He squinted at me. "If you're not a vigilante, then whom are you working for?"

I snorted. "'Working for'. You say that like I get paid. Here's the thing, it doesn't matter whether I have proof or not. With something as dangerous as the Power Suits, I can't afford to take chances. You're a suspect, and every suspect is guilty until proven innocent ... In this case, anyway."

"Well then, if that's the case, I'm afraid you'll have to take me by force." Lincoln's tuxedo singed and burned itself to ashes, revealing the grey Power Suit underneath.

"Wow, you know a guy's rich when he's perfectly okay with burning up a sweet tuxedo like that."

Lincoln responded by charging at me, fist first, which I only narrowly avoided.

He fought like a bull—lots of power and speed, but very little direction. You'd think that wouldn't be a good strategy for a fistfight, but you'd be wrong. He got his arms around me, restricting my movement. His grasp lifted me into the air.

"Quite a grip you've got there," I gasped. I was certain he would have cracked my ribs if my suit's nanobots weren't actively resisting his crushing force.

"I'm aware. I grew up in the slums of this city. Street brawling was practically a rite of passage. It was a steep climb to get where I am today, so don't think for a second that I am ill-prepared to deal with interlopers." I squirmed as he held me out the window. "Try not to scream on the way down." He dropped me, and I fell like a bowling ball.

I flailed, but my suit balanced me (and silenced my screaming). *Claws, Claws, Claws,* I thought frantically, trying to activate them faster. When they finally did activate, I plunged them into the wall and slowed my descent until I stopped.

Immediately, I began my climb back up, grumbling, "When I get back up there, I am so going to … find out that you're not here."

I poked my head through the open window and found the room empty. The X-ray mode on my Visor confirmed it.

Thomas Lincoln had escaped.

The Visor also confirmed something else, a hidden compartment in the floor underneath the bookshelves.

I entered the room and moved the bookshelves out of the way. Opening the compartment, I found some papers—hand-drawn blueprints, they looked like. They were the designs for the Power Suits. I guess that confirms his guilt. Lincoln must have digital copies of this; that's probably what Christine stole from him to get the designs …

I paused then. I couldn't pretend I wasn't worried about Christine any longer. But I also had a job to do. I took a breath.

From what I could understand of the blueprints, the Power Suits used an electrical current to stimulate muscle movement. When they're activated, there's a discharge that scorches off clothing but not skin.

I stored the designs in my suit and headed back to the APD's headquarters.

Chapter 12

Both versions of the Power Suit are still in play as well as both their suppliers, so today's mission is to try and get some of these suits off the streets. And if I'm lucky, maybe I'll get a lead as to where I can find Christine ... I just hope she's okay.

From a rooftop, I stared down at the city, peering into its dark corners in hopes of finding something—anything. The brown-Power-Suit users have been admittedly harder to find, so the police showing up at Christine's hideout must have been a fairly big blow to her operation.

I spent the night patrolling the city, stopping any criminal activity I could find, especially if the perpetrators were wearing Power Suits.

I found a couple of idiots with grey Power Suits who were robbing a convenience store owner at gunpoint. I met them at the door as they dashed out. One of them pointed a gun at me, but I easily plucked it out of his hand.

"I'll take that," I said, unloading it and absorbing it into my suit to dispose of later. "If you're looking to make a return, guys, the owner's in there." I pointed them back toward the shop.

Believe it or not, they actually listened to me. They sighed and walked back into the store to return the money they stole. When they came back out of the store, they just said, "Sorry," and started walking away.

"Uh, hang on, guys," I called after them.

"What?" one of them said. "We didn't do nothing. We gave the money back, so there ain't no issue."

He seemed genuinely confused. "You do realize you still threatened someone at gunpoint, and you're wearing Power Suits, which is illegal?"

They sighed and approached me with their hands ready to be cuffed.

"I knew we shouldn't have bought these stupid suits," one of them mumbled.

I handcuffed them and called the police to come pick them up. But it was when the police showed up that I finally got a break.

A man wearing a brown Power Suit stumbled out of an alleyway, his face bruised and bloodied. He collapsed on the ground when I ran over to him.

"Are you okay?" I asked him, propping him up against a building wall. "What happened to you?"

He took a few shaky breaths. "She's crazy, she's crazy," he kept mumbling. He pointed shakily to the alleyway he came from.

I realize I had no way of knowing this, but at the time, I was convinced he was talking about Christine.

I ushered the police officers over to deal with the man and rushed into the alleyway.

It was like a maze—a dark alleyway that connected to loads of other dark alleyways. I wasn't finding anyone in here; it was empty.

I desperately scaled the nearest wall to search from the rooftops, but I couldn't see anything. There were too many brick walls around; they would make it hard to distinguish any heat signatures with my Visor's Thermal mode. I tried the X-ray mode, but I was seeing more of what was happening inside the buildings than I was behind the walls.

But then there was a yell. "Help!"

It was short, and they didn't yell again, but I had a lead.

I followed the sound, returning to the ground to finally see who I'd been looking for. Christine. Baseball bat in hand, she stood before a brutally beaten woman wearing a brown Power Suit who was pinned to the ground due to her injuries. Blood dripped from her face and Christine's bat alike.

The woman didn't have the strength to acknowledge my arrival. She pleaded with Christine. "Please, boss, I … I'm sorry. I didn't tell Lincoln's guys anything."

Christine responded through gritted teeth. "Make me believe you."

"I ran a job with some of his guys. I needed money. That doesn't mean I'm not loyal. I swear, I didn't tell them anything. I got in, did the job, and got out … Please."

"Christine," I butt in.

Her grip on the bat tightened, but she didn't look at me. "Go away."

"We both know I can't do that."

"Can't or won't?"

I paused. "Christine, I want to help you."

She scoffed and readied her bat to hit the woman. Using my Sticky String, I yanked it from her hand and threw it to the ground. The woman hid her face in fear.

Christine kicked her hard to get her attention, and she almost vomited. "Leave, Ange. Don't disappoint me again."

She nodded, stumbled to her feet, and started running.

Christine's fists tightened. "Leave me alone, Scar."

"I'm trying to help you."

She whipped her gaze to me. Her eyes were red, like she'd been crying. "Really, you're trying to help me?" She said it mockingly.

"I am." I spoke calmly.

She shook her head and scoffed. "Go away, Scar. Go find some other criminal to catch." She turned and started walking away.

"Christine, you know I can't let you leave."

"Why not!" She turned and looked at me. "Just let me go. Stop pretending that you give a shit!"

"Then stop pretending that you don't. Christine, you've gone too far; I'm trying to help you out. Let me help you."

"You want me to give a shit, Alex, is that what you want?"

Whoa. I don't think she's ever called me *Alex* before.

She stormed over to me and pushed me backward. "You left!" she screamed. "It was us, Alex, you and me. We were supposed to be family. But then that guy in the suit showed up and took you away, and I didn't know what happened to you. For all I knew, they locked you up for all the burglaries we pulled together. For all I knew, that bastard might have killed you. I don't even know who he was." She paused, closing her eyes and breathing to hold back tears. "It's like you're a different person now. They might as well have killed you because I don't know who you are anymore."

"I'm sorry, Christine. It's ... complicated."

"What's complicated?" she pushed through gritted teeth.

"The guy in the suit who took me away, he ..." I sighed. "Can you just trust me? What did happen to me isn't ... great. Can you just trust that I'm trying to do what's best for us both? I haven't changed, Christine. We're still partners. We're still family. Trust me. Let me help."

She couldn't stop the tear that fell down her cheek. "How's this for trust?" She put her wrists together and presented them to me. "Just do it. Arrest me or whatever."

I was a little shocked, but I didn't want to hesitate long enough to let her change her mind. I cuffed her quickly.

"You're not going to stop," she continued. "There's only one way this will end: you against me, and, Scar, I don't want to fight that fight. I loved you. I loved what we had. But I'm not going to fight for it. It's gone. Even if I win the fight, I've still lost you. We can't go backward ... so I'm done." She leaned back on the wall and slumped to the ground.

Using the power of my nanobot suit, I contacted the police and explained the situation to them, as well as gave them my location so they could take Christine.

I sat down next to her.

"Is it true my mom killed herself?" she asked me quietly.

I looked at her, questioning with my expression how she got that information.

"Her death was reported on the news," she explained. "They said, 'severe head trauma'. I shook down some of my guys, and they all said they didn't touch her. When the cops swarmed the building, they found her like that, dead."

I nodded. "It looks like she bashed her head into the wall just before the police arrived, yeah."

Christine's expression was unreadable. She was smiling, but she didn't look happy. "I thought ... I don't know. I thought it'd feel different, you know? I thought I'd feel ... something ... something different." Her gaze crept toward the bloody baseball bat on the ground. "Maybe you're right, Scar. Maybe I've gone too far."

She rested her head on my shoulder, and her body tensed, like being near me again was a medicine she didn't want to take.

The police arrived. I helped Christine to her feet and escorted her to them, handing her over to an officer who seated her in the back of a police car. She had her head down the whole time.

I'd broken her, and I didn't know if that was a good thing.

"We've been looking for this one," said the officer, closing the car door. "The dreaded Dog Burglar." She said this with exaggerated gravitas. She must have heard those words on the news or something.

"She needs compassion, not condemnation."

"Tell that to the people killed in her name," the officer laughed.

"I'm serious. She's not well."

The officer straightened up after realizing how serious I was being. She looked at Christine in the car, then she looked back to me. "Yeah, okay. I'll, uh, I'll make sure she's taken care of."

"Thank you."

The officer smiled to herself. "Let he who is without sin cast the first stone, right?" She got into the police car. "You have a good one. And thanks for your help in getting the Dog Burglar off the streets." Then she drove away.

So that's it. The Dog Burglar is finally off the streets, and the city is safer for it. But it doesn't feel like a win, not for me, and not for Christine. She thinks she's lost me, lost us. Is she right? All this time I've been thinking that she needed me to stop her from becoming the worst version of herself, but maybe I needed her, too, to stop me from becoming complacent. How long can I keep all this up with the APD? If I just keep going as is, I can't ever see Christine again, not like before, at least ... Who am I kidding? I know this will all come crashing down on me in the end. As much as I want to ignore it, eventually, I'll have to deal with my *other* problem.

And then what?

Chapter 13

It's been a month since the Dog Burglar was arrested, and I've been spending that time catching her former employees and cleaning up her messes. I've been thinking about her a lot, too, wondering if she's okay. And at the same time, I've been letting myself become complacent again. That's what I do. There's so much darkness in my life, and I just don't want to deal with it. So I ignore it, make jokes. I forget it exists. Christine made me deal with it. I was reminded of that when I arrested her ... maybe I should have heeded that reminder.

It was time.

My heart raced. My veins darkened. My scar turned blood red. I was already on a rooftop, patrolling the city in the dead of night, so I was as far as I could get from innocent people. I could only embrace it. I could only give in and hope that I could go back to ignoring it afterward.

I was now just an onlooker as my body stood and stared at the city below.

My hand was brought into my line of focus.

"Interesting," I said with a deep and demonic voice. "He's acquired some sort of body-enhancing suit." I felt the fabric. "Nanobots. A poor choice. Organic symbiosis is far more efficient than mechanical symbiosis."

I took a deep breath, and I could smell the people below me, like food, like a buffet or a Thanksgiving dinner. It was an intoxicating scent, sweet and savoury at the same time. It invited me in, and at the same time, burdened me.

I was getting ready to leap off the roof and begin my feast, but I stopped. I could hear a steady heartbeat. "What are you doing here?"

Someone from behind, with a voice as deep and demonic as mine, answered the question. "I'd like to show you something."

"I thought you and I were enemies."

"And that means we can't share information?"

I turned and faced the six-foot-tall figure draped in a brown cloak.

"Why do you bother concealing your identity?" I questioned scornfully.

"I've learned from prior mistakes. We are not wholly infallible. This was proven to us in Dimension-002. We waged war on that world, and look what happened. The humans cannot know we are here."

"You overestimate their chances. Sarah was a unique case. No one here has proved a threat to me; they will not survive a full invasion from all of your kind."

"I've been meaning to ask you, how do you possess so much knowledge? Sarah, Project Hybrid, these all began before your birth."

"I have implanted memories of my mother; I imagine they are encoded into my DNA. I know what you did to her, and knowing your species, it wasn't difficult to surmise what you would do with the information you obtained from her."

Well, that answered one question. The *other* me's mother is not my mother. It's some woman named *Sarah*.

"Curious." The figure shrugged subtly. "All the same, we shall not be directly attacking the humans. This world is only required for experimentation."

I chuckled. "Are you that frightened of the interdimensional traveller?"

"Yes," said the figure bluntly. "He's gathering people to fight us, and among them is the hybrid. She single-handedly stopped the invasion of Dimension-002. Imagine what she could do with help, with the traveller's resources. Not to mention the abeedoids are still hunting us. We have enemies everywhere, so we must focus on Project Hybrid. We need it to be operational as soon as possible."

"What about the virus?"

The figure paused.

"I told you, I know what you did to my mother. You are very predictable. Do you expect me to believe that at no point during your study of her DNA did any of you consider biological warfare?"

The figure grunted, almost disappointedly. "We have someone in Dimension-004 working on that, but in the meantime, we need a functioning hybrid army. Our kind will not be truly safe and free until we've eliminated our enemies."

I smiled. "Well then, you seem to have it all figured out. What do you want with me?"

"Follow me."

"So you can lead me into a trap? I don't think so."

"If I wanted you dead, I'd come find you when the human has control of your body. He'd be much easier to kill."

If I had any control, I would have shivered at that. "Even so, of what interest are your experiments to me?"

"The offer to help free you from that body is still on the table, and we may have just had a breakthrough."

I stared at the cloaked figure. I couldn't see the face behind the hood, but I could tell I was really trying to. My stare was penetrating.

"Show me," I said.

The cloaked figure fused with the darkness below, and I followed. We travelled through the nighttime shadows of Neetro City until we reached the outskirts, specifically an open field. We emerged from the shadows and walked onto the dewy grass. Strangely, as we walked, our surroundings began to morph from an open field to an interior hallway made out of stone. It was like the open field was a mirage or something.

"I see you've improved upon your cloaking technology," I said.

"Indeed. This is far more efficient than having to attach our structures to an already existing building. We can place it wherever we like, locked and hidden to anyone who does not possess shadow-blood."

I nodded, walking with my hands behind my back.

The hallway opened up into a much more spacious laboratory. It didn't appear to be in use at the moment, but there were cylindrical containers storing what looked like babies—human babies ... with pitch-black veins ... just like mine. The containers were filled with a clear liquid, and they were attached to computers that seemed to monitor the infants' vitals.

Another cloaked figure approached from the dimly lit surroundings and joined us. From behind its black hood, it grunted.

"You may speak," said the brown-cloaked creature.

"Thank you," the black-cloaked one responded. It walked with us through the laboratory. "Project Hybrid is progressing as planned. We've just brought in a new batch of humans and begun introducing the serum."

"Excellent."

"However, an issue is arising. As we proceed with the experiments, it's becoming more apparent that the formula is flawed. We have been able to ensure a near ninety-eight percent success rate in converting the humans to hybrids, but only forty percent of those humans remain within our control."

"Can this be remedied?"

The black-cloaked creature pondered. "I can devote resources to look into it, but we lack sufficient data to ensure that the problem can be solved. Unfortunately, the faction in Dimension-002 did not send us very much data to go on."

"See to it that this issue is remedied quickly. The last thing we need is for this army to turn on us. We have enough to worry about as it is. Ensure that they remain in our control."

"Yes, sir. On another note, what shall I do with the infertile batch of humans?"

"Dispose of them out back. Cease communication."

The black-cloaked creature nodded and left.

"I wonder if Sarah's innate animosity has something to do with why you're having trouble controlling the hybrids," I suggested.

"Possibly," agreed the brown-cloaked figure. "But even so, we should be able to isolate that part of the genome and remove it."

Someone else was approaching. A naked woman bleeding from various parts of her body stumbled toward me. Her heartbeat was so irregular, like it couldn't decide whether to beat quickly or slowly, and the scent of life within her was only faint. She walked as if in a drunken daze, and she moaned like she was sick with the plague. When close enough, she wrapped her arms around me tightly, but before she could do anything more, I pushed her away with a significant amount of force, and she fell to the ground.

"What is wrong with this one?" I questioned disgustedly.

"I apologize," the figure sighed. "She must have escaped the breeding area. Pay her no mind."

The woman let out a yelp and clutched her stomach. She vomited a mixture of reds and yellows, and then collapsed right into it, face first.

Her heart stopped.

"Well, that's unfortunate," said the figure. "Occasionally our experiments prove fatal to the humans. We lose quite a few that way."

Then it all started to click. The shadow woman I fought a while back, she was like me. Then she died, poisoned by her own DNA ... like the dead woman before me. These creatures, they're the Adultnapper. They're kidnapping people and experimenting on them.

We continued walking, leaving the naked, dead woman on the ground in a puddle of her own vomit.

"Tell me of these experiments," I said. "Do they involve the same means by which I was created?"

"Similar, yes. Project Hybrid was in its infancy when we created you, but we now have a much better handle on the inner workings. We can create an army that is much faster and stronger than are we, and with any luck, perhaps one day they will be superior to the original from which they were made."

"Sarah?" I confirmed.

"Yes. None of our hybrids have been able to match her abilities yet, but they are close." The cloaked figure groaned. "Unfortunately, our experiments have been marred with issues. Most notably, the serum will only work on infants. It is like a virus, but because it is based on Sarah's half-human DNA, it is too similar to that of a normal human, and as such, fully-grown humans are able to easily fight the virus off with their conditioned immune systems. However, the immunity of an infant is not yet fully developed. They are fallible enough for the serum to take hold."

"So where are you acquiring the infants?" I asked.

"We breed them. We capture adult humans with proven fertility and bring them here. We drug them to have them copulate more frequently, and then we experiment on the offspring. The drugs we give the parents decrease gestation time from months to weeks, and the child will grow to adulthood in just thirty-five days. The serum is introduced when the infant is born, and when they grow to adulthood, they are complete."

"Why not have the hybrids themselves reproduce with one another?" I asked. "I imagine that would be more efficient, birthing a child who potentially already has the serum encoded into their DNA."

"Unfortunately, the hybrids are sterile."

I looked at the cloaked figure, confused. "But the first test subject was able to reproduce; that's how I was created."

"Indeed. It's quite the enigma. The first test subject reproduced with a human, so perhaps that made a difference. Alternatively, it's possible that Sarah was infertile from the off or that the issue is with our formula rather than its source. But perhaps it's all for the best. By breeding humans, we are decreasing their number whilst increasing our own, thereby subsuming our enemies."

I nodded. "It is all quite impressive."

This was insane. They're farming human beings. They're capturing people, drugging them, breeding them, and the result is the dead woman behind us, lying naked in her own vomit.

And the *other* me finds it impressive.

"So what does this have to do with me?" I asked.

"You?"

"You said you've had a breakthrough in discovering how to free me from this body."

"So I did. I've been keeping tabs on the human occupying your body. You'll never guess what he does. He appears to be in the business of hunting his fellow humans, specifically, those who pose a threat to the society of this city. Curious. I believe you would qualify as just such a threat. Don't you?"

"Your point being?"

The cloaked figure paused. "I fear I've kept you away from your meal for far too long. I know how hard it is to practise self-control when you are in such dire need of sustenance."

Our surroundings faded, transitioning from the laboratory to a parking lot in the middle of the city. It was dark and raining, but I could still see that the lot was filled with naked and exhausted bodies, scattered on the ground, bruised, bleeding, and vomiting. And every one of them was a person reported missing and/or kidnapped by the Adultnapper.

The worst part was I could smell them ... and they smelled so good.

"I imagine you are famished," said the cloaked creature. "This is the infertile batch, too exhausted to fornicate and therefore useless. Please do enjoy the sustenance. The human's comrades will surely come for you soon."

The cloaked figure disappeared into the shadows.

I could hear their pounding hearts. I could smell the life flowing through them, however faint. This was checkmate for me; I couldn't control myself. I formed shadowy claws over my hands and attacked.

Blood sprayed as I tore these people to pieces and absorbed the life from them through my palms. This was the nightmare I hated. Peeling their flesh like it were a banana peel, pulling their bones from their sockets as if I were separating the wings of a perfectly cooked turkey. I hated knowing what it was like to view human beings like food.

And in the end, all that remained was a pool of blood and the barely recognizable remains of the dead.

A sharp pain shot through my shoulder, and I immediately felt nauseated. I felt my shoulder and pulled out what looked like a mechanical tranquillizer dart. I turned slowly and there was Chloe, shakily pointing a gun at me. Her expression of shock was partially covered by the strands of wet hair in her line of vision, but she was too focused on me to brush them away.

I crushed the tranquillizer dart in my grasp and lunged for her, hearing her beating heart, smelling her life, craving it. But the previous tranquillizer dart had already dazed me, so Chloe had the upper hand. With just two good punches and a kick to the jaw, I fell into the pool of blood I'd created.

She shot me with two more darts for good measure, and before long, everything faded to black.

Chapter 14

My eyes cracked open and locked onto my hands. They moved—I moved them—not the *other* me. I sighed, and my aching muscles felt it.

It was over ... for now.

With that relief aside, I realized that my wrists were strapped to the armrests of a wooden chair with the same handcuffs used to restrain people with enhanced strength. What's more, I wasn't wearing my suit anymore; the wristwatches were gone. I was just in regular street clothes—a plain shirt and pants.

My eyes darted around. I wasn't exactly sure where I was. There wasn't much light in the room, and it was a little hard to make out anything. But I could see Chloe standing before me with her arms crossed.

"Chloe? What's going on?" I began. "What's with the restraints, and where's my suit?"

"Talk," she said very intentionally.

"Uh, I think I need a little context."

"You want context, Scar? Here's context: You're a fricking liar."

Then it hit me. She saw me. She saw the *other* me.

"Okay, okay, wait, I can explain," I said, flustered.

"Can you?" she yelled. "Well here's what it looks like to me. Director Agatha sent me out on patrol, and what did I come across? A parking lot full of all the people who were kidnapped. I saw you there and thought you made a break in the Adultnapper case. And then you killed them, no, you massacred them. You're still covered in their blood. And you know what that makes me think? It makes me think that you're the Adultnapper."

"What! I'm not—Chloe, listen to me, you have this so wrong."

"Then talk. Fast."

"I'm not the Adultnapper. I swear to you, I'm not. But I know who is. They're some kind of alien race ... maybe. I don't know what they're called, but they're the ones kidnapping people. They're breeding them and experimenting on them."

She laughed. "That is such bullshit."

"I'm not lying. They're experimenting on people."

"You expect me to believe that?"

"Well ... given our line of work, yeah, actually."

"Do you think this is funny, Scar?"

"No. Chloe, I'm telling the truth. We have to stop them."

"And who's going to stop you, Scar? Or did you forget that you killed them? That's how I know you're lying; you killed all those people. Your veins were black, your scar was glowing red, you looked like ... you looked like that shadow woman you fought. Clearly, you've been keeping something from us."

"Indeed, he has," said Director Agatha as she stepped into view. Has she been here all this time? "I think it's time you put all your cards on the table, Mister Scar. Or should I call you Mister Peterson?"

I stared at her blankly.

"That is your legal name, isn't it? Alex Peterson of the Peterson family? The same family that went missing ten years ago. The father's body was eventually recovered and confirmed deceased, but the mother and the child were never found. Until recently, that is, when a homeless man matching the description of what we predict an adult Alex Peterson would look like showed up in the back alleys of Neetro City."

"What is she talking about?" Chloe asked me.

"Don't worry, Ms. Chloe, he'll explain it to you. He doesn't have much of a choice now."

"Explain what?" I said. "So I didn't tell you my name. So what? I'm not the Adultnapper. I didn't betray any of you or whatever the hell you think I've done."

"Mister Scar, need I remind you that this is the Assassination Police Department? It is our job to eliminate dangerous individuals." The director stared at me. "If you don't say it, I will."

What is she ...? Wait ... The cloaked figure, it said something to the *other* me. It said my comrades would surely come for me soon. Why would it say that? It was clearly keeping tabs on me; it must have been watching the rest of the APD as well. What would it have seen that would make it say that? The APD hunts dangerous people, so what's the only piece of information that would make them hunt me?

"You knew," I whispered.

"You were foolish to think I didn't. You know what we do here, Mister Scar. Did you really think I didn't know?"

"Know what?" Chloe snapped. "What the hell are you two talking about?"

"The floor is yours, Mister Scar," said the director.

I took a breath. Here goes nothing. "Okay. My scar's not ... normal. I got it at some point when I was young, and I don't fully remember how. I honestly can't tell you who gave it to me or exactly when I got it. All I know is that every now and then, the scar ... activates—it turns red, and it's like I'm possessed by something that needs to kill people to survive. The *other* me, it consumes some sort of energy from its victims. We each get a designated amount of time with my body. I can't control it when I'm possessed, and it can't control me when I'm not. But, Chloe, listen to me, that monster is not me."

She stared at me disbelievingly.

"That's the truth," I reassured. "I swear."

"Why the hell didn't you mention that before? That would have been good to know when you first got here, that you could wake up one day and try to kill all of us."

"What the hell was I supposed to say, 'Hi, my name's Scar, and sometimes, the scar on my face turns red and I kill people'? How do you think that would have gone for me?" I looked to the director. "The real question is: How did you know? Why did you keep me alive if you knew?"

Chloe turned to the director, too, and now all eyes were on her.

"Very well," she said. "Mister Scar, I've had you under close surveillance ever since your *other* half first showed up. You were a dangerous killer, and the APD needed to stop you. But as I continued to watch, I realized you weren't always that monster. You were a completely different person, still a criminal, but nothing that required the APD's attention. Even still, I had to stop the *other* you from attacking again. So I took you in and gave you an ultimatum: Join us, or we kill you. You're not a bad person, Mister Scar. I didn't want to kill you unless I had to. I took you off the streets and gave you an External Nanobot Skin which I had modified to keep your problem at bay. But unfortunately, it didn't work. Your suit was perhaps able to hold it back for a while, but eventually, the monster within was unleashed, and you murdered a great many people tonight."

The room was silent. Chloe shook her head and walked out, disappearing into the bright, white light that burst through the door before it closed behind her.

"So that's it, then," I sighed. "You know. The *other* me can't be stopped. You'll have to kill me."

Director Agatha shook her head. "I can't. You've done a lot for this organization, Mister Scar, and I can't forget that. You're not a bad person, and I don't want to treat you like one." She sighed. "I have one last idea of how to deal with you. I'll be sending you to Viker Island."

"Viker Island? What the hell is that?"

"The location of Neetro City's most prestigious prison."

My heart dropped. "A prison? No, you can't send me to prison. If the *other* me shows up, everyone there will die."

"They are very well equipped to deal with that sort of thing there. They should be able to keep you contained. But if they can't, Mister Scar—and I sincerely hope it will not come to this—we will have no choice but to eliminate you, and that will be the end of it."

The director called Chloe back in using her suit, and when she came to take me away, the look in her eyes reminded me of the look in Christine's eyes when I arrested her.

Chapter 15

The Locker. That's what this prison is called according to the sign outside—four thick walls isolated on a tiny island just off the city coast. It keeps prisoners in and doesn't let them back out (you know, the cliché of every high-security prison out there).

Chloe left quickly after dropping me off. I don't blame her; she probably hates me now.

I was put through the prison equivalent of airport customs. They checked me for weaponry, took my picture, took my fingerprints, took a blood sample (I know, total violation), cleaned me, and made me change into grey prison clothes. After that, lucky me was sent outside because I happened to arrive during the one hour I didn't have to be locked in a cell.

I use the term *outside* very loosely. There was no grass at all (unless all the dirt and rocks were covering it), and there was a brick wall that surrounded the area, likely metres thick and a good thirty feet tall.

I looked at all the people out here. I think I actually put some of them in here; there are definitely a few Power-

Suit users in the mix. Man, I really hope I don't get jumped. Not that it matters. There's only one way this is going to end. Eventually, the *other* me will show up and kill everyone in here, and then someone will be sent in to kill me.

A ginger-haired woman walked up to me and stood with her arms crossed.

"Well, shit," she said.

Upon further inspection, I realized who it was: Christine in prisoner's grey.

Before I could speak, she grabbed my wrist tightly and dragged me to a more remote part of the prison grounds. She pinned me to a wall roughly with her arm to my chest.

"What the hell are you doing in here?" she snapped.

"Nice to see you, too," I remarked.

She slapped me in the face.

"Whoa, ow, okay, no need for violence." I rubbed my cheek.

"Why are you here?" she pressed, holding me to the wall even tighter than before.

"I ... I was accused of being the Adultnapper." I gave her a half-truth. I don't know why I was still keeping the existence of the APD a secret.

"Are you?" she asked me seriously.

"What? Of course not."

"Not you, dumbass, the *other* you."

"No." I paused. "But I think the *other* me knows the people who are."

"People? More than one?" she questioned.

"I think so, yeah."

She sighed. "That goddamn scar is always getting you into trouble."

"Don't I know it? Um, can you let me go now; you're kind of hurting me."

"Oh, sorry." She smiled and removed her arm from my chest. "Got carried away."

We were both silent for a second.

"So," I began, "how, uh, how are you doing?"

She shrugged. "You know. I've been going through some things with a psychiatrist, exercising, trying to keep out of trouble. It's not so bad."

"Good. I'm glad." I shuffled a bit. "Christine, you know, I'm sorry."

"Me, too."

"I think, you know, after we were separated, we both made some questionable decisions, and it's kind of created a rift between us."

"It has." She nodded.

"But I don't want us to be weird. We're family."

She hugged me slowly and whispered into my ear, "I missed you."

"You, too," I whispered back.

When she pulled away, she looked at me thoughtfully. "Thank you," she said.

"For what?"

"Not giving up on me. You were right. I went too far; I became someone I wasn't. Thank you for stopping me."

"Don't mention it, Puppy."

She smiled and playfully punched my shoulder, stepping over to lean beside me against the wall.

"I've still got to figure out how to escape this place, though," I mentioned.

"Escape?" She looked at me. "What do you mean 'escape'? You just got here."

"Think about it, Christine. The minute the *other* me shows up, it's game over. Everyone in this prison is dead. I have to at least try to escape, for the sake of everyone in here."

She sighed, realization colouring her face. "Right. It's just … I just got you back. I don't want to lose you again."

I looked at her; her eyes were glued to the ground. "Well, maybe … maybe you come with me. I mean, technically, we've always been criminals on the run. We'd just be going back to how life used to be, just with much larger crimes over our heads."

She smiled at me. "I'd like that. I hope you have a good escape plan, though. This is no easy place to get out of. Not only is the prison itself full of safeguards, but it's also on Viker Island. The only connection this place has to the mainland is the boat that transfers prisoners, and it's heavily guarded."

I paused, looking at all the other prisoners here. "I may have something in mind."

"Shoot."

"Are any of your Dog Burglar buddies in here?"

"A few, yeah."

"Are they still loyal to you?"

She grinned. "I can make them loyal. Why?"

The plan was getting clearer in my head. "Do you know the tried-and-true way to create chaos in a prison?"

"A riot," she answered confidently.

"Right. And you already have built-in connections with the people who are going to help us start one. Chaos and confusion are great tools for sneaking around unnoticed."

"And that will buy us the distraction we need to try and sneak out," she finished. "That might work, but we don't know much about the safeguards put in place here. We'll have to stay on our toes."

It was then, when we were both starting to settle back into our renewed relationship, that I changed my mind. I didn't want to keep things from her anymore.

"Uh, Christine."

"Yeah?" She looked at me curiously.

"I want to tell you the truth ... about what happened to me. But listen, Christine, you can't say a word of what I tell you to anyone. Our lives kind of depend on it."

She didn't look away. "I'm listening."

I took a breath. "All right. The guy in the suit who took me away was actually an agent of an organization called the Assassination Police Department or APD." I paused to gauge her reaction, but she didn't really react. "The

APD is a secret division of the Neetro City Police that deals with criminals who are too dangerous for the regular police to handle."

"So what, they kill them?" she asked.

"When there's no other choice, yeah. When they took me in, I was given an ultimatum: Join them or they kill me."

"Why? You're not a dangerous criminal."

"I'll get to that. At the time, they said it was because I knew about their organization. I couldn't leave with that information. I didn't know where I was or how to leave, but my plan was to just play along with them, and eventually, they had to let me leave their headquarters and patrol the city. That's when I was going to look for you."

"So why didn't you?"

I paused. "I didn't want you to have to make the same decision I had to make. I was afraid that you wouldn't put up with their crap, and they'd try to kill you. So I thought it would be better if I didn't find you."

This was the first time she looked away.

"As it turns out," I continued, "the real reason they took me in is because they knew about the *other* me. They'd seen me, and to them, I was a dangerous threat who needed to be killed. But they also saw that I'm not always that monster. So their plan to get me off the streets was to force me to work for them, and that suit I wore, that was meant to keep the *other* me away. But it didn't work. I told you I was in here because I was accused of being the Adultnapper, but that's only half true. I'm in here because I'm dangerous, and if the *other* me shows up in here, and they can't stop me—which they won't be able to—then they'll kill me."

Christine was silent.

"That's it. That's what happened."

"Christine," a woman called as she approached us.

"That's my doctor," Christine explained. "I've got to go. We'll regroup tomorrow, okay?"

"Okay."

She kissed me and said, "Thank you ... And try not to die in here while I'm gone."

I smiled. "No promises."

As she regrouped with her doctor, I couldn't help overhearing their conversation. Guess I didn't need my suit to still utilize the acute senses gained from all my APD training.

"Who was the man you were with, Christine?" the doctor started.

"That's Scar."

"I see. Is he the one you were telling me about?"

"That's the one."

"You seem to care very deeply for him, if you don't mind me saying."

Christine paused. "Yeah, I really do."

Chapter 16

The next day—around the same time as the last—Christine and I found ourselves outside, standing with folded arms in front of a man who was seated on the ground and chucking a few pebbles around. We put up a rather intimidating front, but he didn't seem fazed.

"What the hell are you looking at, Summers?" he drawled.

Christine answered. "I have a job for you."

The man laughed hysterically. "You can't be serious."

"I'm dead serious."

"Then I hate to break it to you, but I don't think your doctors are doing such a bang-up job." He pointed at me. "If you think any of your old employees are going to listen to you after the fiasco with this guy kicking the shit out of you—and he's apparently your fricking friend now—then you're clearly still psycho."

I grinned when Christine crouched down to his level. This was going to be fun.

She punched him right in the face and then grabbed him by the collar and pulled him in; he didn't even have time to nurse his wound.

"Ah, hell!" he spat, blood pouring out of his nose and onto Christine's hand, not that she cared.

"Now you listen to me," she started. "Number one: Don't call me psycho. Number two: Don't mouth off about shit you don't understand. And number three: When I tell you to do something, you do it." She threw him on the ground and wiped her bloody hand on her clothes.

"Goddamn it, Summers, why do you have to be so violent?"

"You get used to it," I commented.

Christine frowned at me and shook her head. I guess she wanted me to shut up.

She looked at the man. "I'm sure you remember what happens to puppies who don't follow the pack."

And then he froze. "I'm sorry, boss, I-I didn't realize ... What do you need me to do?"

"I need a riot started. I've already told the others to add to the chaos when they see it, but I need you to start the fire."

"You got it, boss. When do you want it for?"

"Tomorrow. I'll tell you when." The man nodded, and Christine continued. "I'll also be needing your thievery skills."

"Sure." He grinned. Clearly, thievery was a skill he was proud of.

"I need you to get a paperclip from my property bag, and I need it by tomorrow. Can you do that?"

"Easy."

"Good. And, Tim ..."

"Yeah?"

"Don't ever disrespect me like that again, or I'll give you way worse than a bloody nose."

The man bowed his head. "Won't happen again."

Christine and I left him to clean up his nose.

"What's the paperclip for?" I asked her as we walked.

"There's a good chance there'll be some locked doors when we try to escape, right? We'll need something to pick locks with."

"True. I'm surprised you got all your Dog Burglar pals to obey you so easily."

"I trained them to." She smiled smugly.

"You trained them to?"

"Yeah. I've conditioned all of them to associate certain phrases with pain and fear. I may be good at what I do, but I don't look that intimidating. Tools like that help me to control the pack."

"You mean *helped*. This is only temporary, Christine. You're not the Dog Burglar anymore."

She smiled at me. "I know. Once we do this, we can both go back to how things used to be. No more criminal underworld, no more crime-fighting, just you and me roughing it on the streets."

I chuckled. "That should not sound as enticing as it does."

She grinned and put her arm around me. "No, it shouldn't."

***

One day soon rolled over into the next, and when the time to be outside returned, Christine and I reacquainted ourselves with our little riot starter.

"You ready, boss?" he asked.

"Not so fast," Christine said. She put out her hand. "Paperclip."

"Oh, right." He started heaving and thumping his chest with his fist until he successfully hacked up a paperclip. He presented the saliva-covered tool to Christine.

"Wipe," she demanded.

He cleaned the paperclip on his prison clothes and presented it again.

Christine took it and said, "Good boy. Now get to work."

"Yes, ma'am." He nodded and left.

Christine looked at me. "Okay. When he starts the riot, the others will join in and make it bigger. When it's big enough, the prison guards will surely come to stop it, and we can escape from the entrance they use."

"How are we going to do that?" I questioned. "Won't there be prison guards, you know, guarding the entrance?"

"What, are you afraid of some prison guards?"

"No, but they'll definitely make things harder."

She looked at me. "Do you even know who you're talking to, Scar? I know how to kick someone's ass if I need to, and so do you. You held your own against me for a little longer than I expected."

"But we both had strength-enhancing suits on."

"We'll be fine."

Before anything else could be said on the matter, the prison exploded into a sea of yelling and violence, and a battle royal had begun almost instantaneously. As riots go, it was quite impressive, and it wasn't long before a metal door connecting to the prison interior burst open, and out swarmed three prison guards dressed in white, insulated suits and armed with metal staffs that looked to have powerful electric currents surging through them.

"All prisoners are ordered back to their cells!" one of them yelled. "Non-compliance will be punished!"

Christine and I ran toward the metal door and rushed the guards. And once we did, some of Christine's old employees rushed them as well. We outnumbered them, and they swung their staffs at us wildly. I still had my sixth sense, so the fight wasn't too difficult for me. However, without my suit, it was much harder to manoeuvre the way I used to. Luckily, Christine's employees took most of the hits for us, giving us a chance to slip away through the door.

We ran down the murky corridors. There were flashing red lights and sirens, signalling for everyone to return to their cells. We didn't stop running until reaching a crossroads with three possible paths to take.

"Which way?" I asked Christine, as she mulled over the options.

"I'm thinking," she said.

"You do know your way around here, right?"

"What would make you think I know my way around?"

"Because you've been in here longer than me."

"What, and that means I have the prison blueprints memorized? I wasn't even planning on getting out of here until you showed up."

"Well, we have to hurry. I'm sure those guards aren't that far behind."

"Don't worry; we'll just wing it. Let's go left." She ran in that direction before I could even argue the point, and I reluctantly followed.

We continued this method of taking random turns and trying to map the place out in our heads until we reached a massive, metallic double door with a padlock.

"Well, this kind of looks like an exit." Christine smiled.

"I hope so," I said, amazed that she wasn't out of breath from all the running, and a little disappointed that I was.

"I'll need time to pick the lock," she said. "Cover me."

"Will do." I stood with my back to her, staring down the gloomy corridor. "You know, I'm surprised a place like this is using a padlock as security. I would have thought they'd use an eye scanner or something."

"They probably do," said Christine. "I hear the warden's a big fan of multiple levels of security. You may get a lot of people in here who are good at hacking into digital locks but have no clue how to pick an old-fashioned padlock. So he uses both. Don't worry, I'm sure this won't be the only door we'll have to get through."

Then, from around the corner, a much larger prison guard appeared. He stood about seven feet tall. He was also wearing a white, insulated suit and armed with an electrified staff proportional to his size.

"Prisoners, return to your cells," he said with a somewhat robotic voice.

"How about, I give you five bucks, and you pretend you never saw us?" I quipped.

I could hear Christine giggling behind me.

The prison guard stepped forward resolutely and brandished his staff.

"All right, suit yourself." I shrugged. "I'm broke anyway."

He lifted the staff over his head and slammed it down like a mallet, but my sixth sense warned me, and I jumped out of the way. The ground shook a little when the staff struck. Without my suit, there wasn't much I could do to stop him. I could only try to stall until Christine got the door unlocked.

The guard lunged his staff toward me, and I evaded. I may not have had my suit anymore, but I think my muscles were starting to warm up. It was getting a little easier to move as fast as my sixth sense demanded.

Then Christine said, "Got it! Let's go." And we both ran through the door and down a new corridor. We could run a lot faster than the guards here. I guess their insulated suits slowed them down. I was pretty relieved about that; I didn't think I could hold my own against them for long. But my relief turned out to be premature. Christine and I were stopped in our tracks when we ran into an outdoor area that seemed to connect two parts of the prison together, and those parts were separated by a moat, and there were a few signs around the area warning that the water was electrified.

Christine and I both stared at the sight blankly.

"You know, I don't think we fully thought this plan through," I pointed out. "For a place called Viker Island, we should have guessed there would be some sort of water-based security around."

"I kind of imagined we could hijack one of the transfer boats," Christine responded, awestricken by the sight. "I didn't even realize this prison was split into two sections."

"Yeah, admittedly, this is not our brightest moment."

We both sighed as we were swarmed by prison guards who took our hands behind our backs and cuffed us.

Chapter 17

With our plan failed and our hopes of escape crushed, Christine and I were brought into a windowless room with just one door. The prison guards who'd brought us here tied Christine and me to separate metal chairs. There was a tiny lightbulb struggling to keep the room lit, though it was blocked out by one of the prison guards standing before us.

He spoke with a robotic voice. "The warden will be with you shortly."

"Correction," said a voice from just outside the open door. "The warden will be with you *immediately*."

The guard moved out of the way, and the pale and fragile-looking man came into view.

"So, these are the two escapees." The warden adjusted his circular glasses and looked at us disapprovingly. "The pair of you aren't very intelligent, are you? Pathetic little cretins. You thought you could escape my prison with nothing more than pluck and optimism? The Locker, by my design, is inescapable. There has only ever been one person who was able to escape these walls, and frankly, neither one of you are as capable as he. The two of you shall remain here for as long as the legal system allows."

"Look," I interrupted. "You don't understand. We—"

"Did I say you could speak?" he snapped.

"Um ... no."

"Correct. And that would be because I have not permitted it." The warden paced back and forth. "I own this island, and I can make revisions to it as I see fit. I'm the richest man in this whole bloody city."

"Tell that to Thomas Lincoln," Christine commented.

The warden walked over to her and slapped her across the face. "I don't recall asking to hear your prattling."

"You didn't have to hit her," I said.

"Oh, shut up." He continued pacing. "No one asked for your whinging either."

I looked over at Christine. Her cheek was red, and she looked at the warden with intense hatred in her eyes. If she weren't restrained, I knew she'd put this guy in his place.

"I am constantly improving the security of this prison," the warden continued, "and for that reason, and that reason alone, no one will ever escape. Even if your ridiculously ill-conceived plan had worked, even if you'd managed to traverse the electrified moat, there would have been many other barriers for you to overcome— fingerprint scanners, laser beams, archers." He grinned.

Another prison guard entered from outside. This one didn't have a robotic voice. "Warden."

"What?"

"Agent Johnson would like a moment of your time."

"Oh, for God's sake, not that prat again. Tell him to wait until I'm finished here."

"I'm afraid he insisted, sir."

The warden sighed. "Send him in."

The prison guard left and re-entered with a serious-looking man in a suit. I immediately recognized him as an APD agent, the same one who recruited me into the APD all that time ago.

"What do you want, agent?" The warden scowled.

"Nice to see you, too, Viker," Agent Johnson greeted.

"If you don't mind, agent, I'm rather preoccupied at the moment."

"Well then, I promise not to take up too much of your time. I'll just need you to return Scar to the APD's custody, and I'll be on my way."

Everyone stared at the agent, shocked. Why would they want me back?

"You're joking," said the warden. "He's a dangerous criminal."

"Maybe not. There was a television broadcast a few hours ago hosted by a cloaked man claiming the identity of the Adultnapper. I trust you saw it?"

"I did." There was a lot of resentment in the warden's voice.

"Then you know that he admitted to kidnapping and using people for experimentation to develop some sort of drug and that he's released the altered people out into the city on a murderous rampage?"

"I'm well aware of the current predicament." The warden paused. "Even if we assume that Scar was telling the truth and he isn't the Adultnapper, it still doesn't change the fact that he is dangerous. I was informed that he can turn into a murderous monster, and despite my wealth, agent, my resources cannot extend into the mainland. If he turns in the city, he'll be liable to join the rampage."

"We'll keep an eye on him. The city is in crisis, and we need all the help we can get. It doesn't matter what he did or who he is, as long as he can help us now. We'll deal with the rest later."

"Fine," the warden seethed, making a hand gesture signalling for one of the prison guards to come free me from the chair.

"I've got to say, Johnson," I said, standing and approaching the APD agent, "I didn't expect the APD to take me back, not after how things ended."

"We're not taking you back," he informed me plainly. "We just need your help. Afterward, you're coming straight back here. Are you willing to comply with that?"

Oh, I so wanted to say *no*. That was the worst deal ever, do something for us and we'll do absolutely nothing for you. But I've seen the experiments those aliens are doing; I've seen what can happen when those people are set loose. I can't just ignore it. I've got to make the right choice ... that's what my mom would have wanted me to do.

"Yeah, I'll comply," I said. "When we're done, you can send me back here, no questions asked."

He returned my wristwatches to me. "Good. And by the way, it's *Agent* Johnson."

"Oh. Well, in that case, I'm pretty sure I'm technically *Agent* Scar."

"Don't push it."

I sighed and put the watches on, activating the skin-tight, nanobot suit. It felt kind of good to be back in my work duds.

"I'll need the girl as well." Agent Johnson pointed to Christine.

"No," I said.

"You're insane," the warden concluded.

"She could be helpful," Agent Johnson explained. "This is a desperate situation, and she has proven capable of handling herself against one of our agents before. We need all the help we can get."

"Well then, by all means, poach my entire prison if you must. Let's just give all the convicts a taste of the outside world again." The warden rolled his eyes.

"If things get bad enough, I might just have to take you up on that." Agent Johnson grinned, but the warden didn't seem to appreciate the joke. "Relax, Viker, we'll send them both back to you when we're done."

"I don't think you understand, agent. Christine Summers is one of the most dangerous people in this prison, in no small part due to her ability to assert dominance and control over others. Give her enough time and she'll turn this entire prison against you. That is the only reason her incredibly ill-conceived escape plan got as far as it did. She has a killer instinct. She lives in a world of 'I kill you before you so much as wound me.' I mean, look at her, for God's sake. She hasn't looked away from me this entire time; you can feel the venom in her eyes. I'm afraid, agent, if you think you can control her once she is released into your custody, you are sorely mistaken."

"I'll take my chances. This isn't my first rodeo. Remember Red?"

"Wait, what?" I said. "Did you just say Red?"

My question was ignored as the warden made another gesture for the prison guards to free Christine. She stood up slowly, eyed everyone in the room, and then launch her fist into the warden's face. The warden fell back a bit, and the prison guards pointed their electrified staffs at her, but she had her hands up, surrendering.

The warden wiped blood from his mouth. "Fair play, girl, though you are only proving my point further. For your sake, you'd better hope you find a way to weasel out of coming back here, because if I do see your face here again, I'll make you regret that last act with every fibre of your being."

Christine didn't respond. She just stepped over to my side with a smile on her face.

Agent Johnson handed her two wristwatches. "Put these on and tap the faces—first right, then left."

Christine looked at me, and I nodded.

She put on the watches and activated them, and a black, skin-tight, nanobot suit formed around her. She seemed a little unnerved by the way the nanobots scurried onto her like ants. "Whoa, this does not feel like other Power Suits."

"That's because it isn't," Agent Johnson explained. "It's an External Nanobot Skin or ENS for short. It uses nanobot technology to improve muscle mass, reflexes, balance, and a number of other things.

"Now, Ms. Summers, I will be escorting you to The Room, where you'll be given a crash course on the suit's major functions and how best to utilize them. It won't take long."

Christine looked at me again, unsure. I gave her another nod, though I wasn't sure how reassuring it was.

"Anyway," the warden chimed in. "I think it's time you were leaving now, agent, and I'd thank you to not return here any time soon."

"Nice seeing you, too, Viker."

The warden grimaced and exited the room.

"Scar," began Agent Johnson. He retrieved a white card from up his sleeve and handed it to me. "That's for you."

The card had an address and my name scribbled on it, as well as a few black blotches, as if someone had spilled ink on it.

"Who's this from?" I asked.

"Mirror-Mind. Chloe found it with a broken wristwatch attached to a dead body on the street."

"How do you know it's from Mirror-Mind?"

"The black stains on the card. We tested them, turns out it's his blood."

"Blood? But it's black."

Agent Johnson looked at me seriously. "Exactly."

I knew of only one way a person could have pitch-black blood, but at this moment, I was really hoping there was another, simpler, not-terrifying explanation.

"Both of your suits have GPS trackers in them," said Agent Johnson to Christine and me. "If you try to bolt, we'll know."

"Don't worry," I said, staring at the card. "I'm not going anywhere."

Chapter 18

After following the address on the card, I arrived at an old, worn-down warehouse. It was isolated away from the other buildings in the city but not to the extent of being out of place. It looked abandoned; there was graffiti everywhere.

I'd like to say that the warehouse was the reason for my thoughts running a marathon, but honestly, there were a multitude of reasons for that, and none of them were about the destination. In the heart of Neetro City, a war was being waged. All the missing people have been released to the public with a strange mutation of some sort—a lot like the *other* me, complete with shadow powers and a tendency to kill people. I want to be helping to protect civilians from these mutated people, but I can't. I have to deal with Mirror-Mind, who was dangerous enough before, but judging from the black blood stains on his card, I've got a feeling he's just become a whole lot worse. I'm all alone this time as well; everyone else is busy dealing with the rampage. And by *everyone*, I also mean

Christine. In spite of everything I have to worry about, I'm most worried for her.

A familiar mountain of a man suddenly stopped my train of thought. Thomas Lincoln approached the warehouse with his hands behind his back.

"Well, if it isn't the guy who's too good to live on the ground floor," I greeted. "How's it hanging?"

"Hmm, I didn't realize this was a group gathering," he commented.

"I'm guessing you got an invite, too?"

"Indeed." He eyed me curiously. "Perhaps there's a reason beyond coincidence as to why Mr. Kennedy wishes to see us both."

"Wow, you even know his name? Studied, did you?"

"It was on the invitation."

"Really? All I got was my name, an address, and some black stains."

He looked at the abandoned warehouse. "I suggest a temporary truce. We don't know what Mr. Kennedy has in store for us, so we'd do well to combine forces."

"I'm sorry, maybe I didn't hear you right. Hero? Villain? Together? This strange concept hurts my head."

He responded with a bored expression.

"All right, fine," I said. "We're partners. As long as you know that when we're done here, I'm having you arrested."

"It will be a pointless effort. I've been arrested before; nothing ever sticks. You're welcome to try, though."

I smiled. "As long as we understand each other."

We walked around the warehouse, looking for a side entrance (didn't want to be too conspicuous when a murderer is expecting us). When we found one, and after discovering it was locked, I briskly kicked it open.

"Ah, I missed you, External Nanobot Skin." I looked at my ally *pro tem*. "Evil business dudes first."

He said nothing and entered the warehouse.

"It wouldn't kill you to say *thank you*," I grumbled.

We walked through the gloomy warehouse. There were stacked wooden boxes and crates all over the place, some of which were stained with blood—both black and red.

"Well, this place isn't inviting at all," I said. "What kind of party is this? I mean, put up some balloons or something."

Lincoln remained silent.

"Oh, sorry. Do you not know what a party is? Sometimes I forget how uptight you businesspeople can be. A party is—"

"I'm well aware of the concept." His response came slowly through gritted teeth.

"Okay, good. So, tell me, is there some rule against throwing a party in the world of lawbreakers?"

He sighed but did not respond.

"Okay, I'll take that as a *classified* and move on. Why do you think Mirror-Mind wanted both of us here? Maybe it's a trap. Or recruitment. Or maybe he just wants to surrender. That would be great. Probably won't happen, though. My money's on the trap."

"My god, do you ever stop talking?" Lincoln scowled.

"Well, I do like to give my voice a break on Tuesdays, but other than that, it's in full swing. Why do you ask?"

He groaned. "If you must speak, can you at least cut out the mindless chatter?"

"Look, I'm just trying to lighten the mood," I levelled with him.

"That's not necessary."

"Come on, you can't tell me you're not a little unnerved that we're likely walking into a trap set by a mass murderer."

"On the contrary, I invite any who think they can best me to try, as long as they know that they'd better not fail." He cracked his knuckles just by clenching his fists. Then he sped up his walking speed so that I was trailing behind him.

The next couple of minutes were spent trying to navigate the warehouse and figure out where Mirror-Mind could be hiding. With all the boxes and crates around, it felt like a maze. Though, soon, we reached the heart of the warehouse, and that's where we met our host.

Mirror-Mind stood still and kept his eyes trained on us. His vest, which was previously a very dirty white, was now stained with small patches of blood—black and red. His skin was covered in jagged black lines, like tree branches, or maybe lightning. My fears were confirmed.

He looked like the *other* me. Those creatures must have gotten to him somehow.

"Oh, look," said Mirror-Mind, smiling at us. "Both my guests have arrived at the same time. That's good. I hoped you would come; I needed an audience."

"An audience?" I questioned. "For what?"

My reserved ally piped up. "Never mind that. I was lured here under the pretense that Mr. Kennedy is in possession of information that would prove compromising for my endeavours."

"Yes, quite the scandal, I thought," Mirror-Mind mused. "I hope she was pretty."

"Why do you want us here so badly?" I butt in. "Why are we so special?"

"I told you before," he looked me right in the eye, "you are very special. And I think we've become good friends, don't you?"

"Sure, it's a real cat-and-dog friendship."

He smiled. "That's what makes it special, how unlikely it is. All my friends die, in the end. But not you. You've lived, and with any luck, you'll outlive me. But as for Mister Thomas Lincoln, some things are set in stone."

"What's that supposed to mean?"

"Boy, you ask a lot of questions. Do I look like an encyclopedia to you?"

"Now there's something we can agree on," Lincoln chimed in. He approached Mirror-Mind. "I don't know how much of what you say is true—"

"Everything I say is true ... unless it isn't," he interrupted.

"Even still, you are a nuisance I'd like dealt with."

"Oh, you want to skip to the main event? Okay." Mirror-Mind raised his hand, calling forth what looked like a shadow but liquefied. He propelled the mass toward Thomas Lincoln, and it engulfed him like water from a fire hose, knocking him to the ground. Then the shadowy liquid hardened around him, making sure he remained grounded.

I tried to help, but I couldn't move. The same shadowy substance was around my feet and hands, preventing me from acting.

"I'm sorry about the restraints," Mirror-Mind said to me. "What happens here is crucial. I can't let you tamper with anything." He crouched over Lincoln.

"So, you went through all the trouble of getting me here just to kill me," said my fearless ally.

Mirror-Mind laughed. "Trouble? Compared to everything I've had to do in my life, getting you here was easy. And necessary. You see, ever since I got these powers, I've had the urge to eat people." He grinned. "Not in the traditional sense, either; I just want to suck the life out of you. I have to test it. I need to know what it feels like."

He wrapped his hands carefully around Lincoln's neck and absorbed some sort of yellow vapour from him. It was like how the *other* me eats people, but this was somewhat different. Mirror-Mind was so careful and intentional as Lincoln's body shrivelled underneath him, pale and lifeless.

"So the tendency toward violence can be avoided," he said. He stood and looked at me. "I think I'll be able to counteract it. That's good for you."

"What the hell are you talking about?" I spluttered, my eyes constantly flitting over to Thomas Lincoln's corpse.

"You'll get there soon. Come with me. I want to show you something."

The shadows surrounding my feet dragged me forward, forcing me to walk wherever Mirror-Mind was taking me. We went deeper into the warehouse to a small area with a wooden table full of beakers and vials. It looked like a little chemistry lab. There was also a small TV on the ground, and with the aid of multiple extension cords, it was on and showing the Neetro City News.

Mirror-Mind approached the table and pulled a knife from his pocket, slitting his hand and letting his black blood drip into one of the beakers. It mixed with the liquid already in it and turned red.

"What is this place?" I asked.

"My home ... for now, at least. I had to leave my home a very long time ago, and I've been a traveller ever since." He bent down and took something from underneath the table. "Here's what I wanted to show you." He walked over to me and showed me a wooden walking stick with an engraving of a timepiece at the top.

I just stared at him blankly.

"I couldn't get my watch working again," he continued. "I've had it for a long time, so I guess it was bound to break eventually. But I stripped out its innards and put them into this wooden cane, hence the engraving of a timepiece at the top—a little reminder of how it began. You never know. I'm only getting older; I might need a cane in the future."

He walked back over to the table to put his walking stick away, and I struggled to move. The shadows were still around my hands and feet like glue.

"I don't suppose you're planning on letting me go any time soon?" I asked.

"In a bit. But first, wouldn't you like to know how I got these powers?"

"Sure. I'm up for a good monologue." I figure if he's talking then he's not killing; that'll buy me time. To do what? I don't know yet.

He approached, standing just a few feet away. "I was taken by the Adultnapper—some guy in a brown cloak with a really deep voice. He took me to a place filled with naked people—half dead, drugged ... like zombies." He took a long, indulgent breath and then stepped back a bit. "I'm sorry, I can't get too close. The pull of your life force is strong. The hardest thing about this is to resist." He smiled to himself. "I don't know how she does it."

"How who does what? What are you talking about?"

But he didn't answer my question. "I don't want to kill you, but I think I understand her a little better now ... and you, and all of them."

He pinched his nose for a second and then continued. "I teleported away from the cloaked man and had a look at some of his research ... and took some of his drugs."

"Wait, what? You just took some of the drugs?"

"How else was I going to know what it was like? Now I can understand it; I can work with it. I'm close, very close."

"But those drugs ... they're only supposed to work on babies. How did they affect you?"

"I altered the formula."

"You altered the formula?" I repeated. "Just like that?"

He grinned. "Just like that."

Who was this guy? This lunatic has just casually made cybernetic enhancements to his body, and now he's talking about altering a formula created by aliens to do things those same aliens couldn't even get it to do.

I was about to question him some more, but my attention was suddenly drawn to the television. It was showing a news broadcast about the murderous rampage happening in the heart of the city.

"This is Jazmine Humble, Neetro City News, reporting live at Neetro City Square." The reporter on the screen looked a bit shaky. I didn't blame her; there was a war raging behind her, and she had the guts to report it live.

A worried whisper sounded from the television, maybe the cameraman. "Jaz, we shouldn't be here. This is dangerous."

The reporter shushed the voice and continued. "As you can see behind me, the city is being attacked by creatures that appear human at first glance, but upon a second look, you'll see that they are quite different."

"Jaz, come on," said the whisperer again. "This isn't worth a couple of college credits."

The reporter put her finger to her mouth, hushing the voice again. She continued. "These creatures are primarily characterized by their stark, black veins. They are extremely agile, powerful, and appear to have the ability to create tangible objects out of shadows." Then she began to tremble; the colour drained from her skin. "T-Tristan"—she pointed—"b-behind you."

There was a scream, and the camera dropped to the ground. I could only see the reporter's feet as they slowly backed away and then broke into a sprint. But she couldn't escape. Another pair of feet, covered in those stark, black veins, pursued her. After another sharp scream, the camera was splattered in her blood, and all I could see was red.

"Well, doesn't that look entertaining?" Mirror-Mind smiled at the TV. "I think I'll go down there and join them."

"Wait," I blurted out.

"Wait? For what?"

Good question. "You ... you don't have to do this. You have power. I'm not just talking about the power you got from those drugs; I'm talking about your intelligence. Clearly, you're really smart. You made all those modifications to your body." Time to grasp at straws. "You don't have to use the power you have to hurt people. You always have a choice."

He looked at me and said something I wasn't expecting. "Sometimes, there is no choice. Sometimes the ability to choose is a privilege you give to others by sacrificing it for yourself."

For the first time in my life, I was lost for words.

"This is a very crucial moment," he continued. "There's only one way this *must* go, and you can't stop it."

Then he raised his hand, and the shadows around my hands and feet disappeared. I instantly launched my Sticky String in his direction, but it only made contact with the ground. Mirror-Mind had fused with the shadows and escaped.

Chapter 19

It wasn't until I arrived at Neetro City Square that I realized the full extent of the situation. The streets were painted red, stained with the blood of the victims. And the ones who trudged through that blood were none other than an army of people affected by the shadow curse. I understood how they felt; they couldn't control their bloodlust. But they'll destroy the city, and the only defence we have is the APD.

Even Christine was here. She was fighting six of these infected shadow people and doing quite well. Whenever the shadow people got too wounded, they would just fade into the shadows and regroup. One of them was heading for Christine, about to slash her in the back of the head with monstrous, shadowy claws. I used my Sticky String to hold back the attacker, and Christine took the opportunity to counter, forcing the enemy to retreat to the shadows.

"Thanks," she said.

"No problem," I chuckled. "You seemed totally lost without me."

"You wish." She hugged me but let me go quickly. We were on a battlefield after all.

Avoiding an attack, Chloe backflipped into view. "Hey, rookie, less talking, more fighting."

"Chill, I just got here," I responded.

"I was talking to Christine," she said sharply, avoiding another attack.

"Just giving away my name, huh?"

She didn't answer. Guess I can't blame her. She probably hates me, and we don't really have time to hash things out right now.

Chloe blocked an attack, creating an opening, then Red arrived to exploit it.

"Thanks for the assist," said Chloe.

"Maybe if you weren't talking so much, you wouldn't need an assist." Red grimaced. Though, he always looked like that, so it was hard to tell.

"Fine, I won't thank you next time."

That was a bit icy. I wonder what happened with them. Did they have an argument? Was it about how things were left with me and the APD?

"Scar," said Red. At least he still seemed interested in talking to me. "Please tell me you're here because you killed Mirror-Mind."

"Killed Mirror-Mind ... well, funny story about that—"

"I'll take that as a *no*. Why are you here, then?"

"He escaped. He saw all this on the news and decided to come down here. Question is: where?"

Christine tapped my shoulder and pointed to the very centre of Neetro City Square. "Does that answer your question?"

She was pointing at Mirror-Mind, who was calmly walking down the street, seemingly oblivious to the warzone around him.

"I'd better go, then," I said.

"I'm coming, too," Christine demanded.

"No, I don't think so."

"I wasn't asking."

I could tell from the look on her face that I wasn't going to win this argument.

I sighed. "Come on."

We ran toward Mirror-Mind, our Claws helping us to easily deal with any shadow people that got in our way. Hopefully, this would be the last time we had to deal with Mirror-Mind. This had to end.

"Well, hello again," he said when we reached him. We were a small distance away, and he looked at us very calmly, hands in his pockets. "You know, part of me hoped you wouldn't come, 'cause I can tell you now, this won't end well."

"That's up to you," I said. "You can end this. You can choose to stop, do your time—"

"Where? The Locker? If you're hoping this will end without death, then I think you're in the wrong business. I've escaped Viker Island three times already. They won't hesitate to kill me if I step foot in there again."

"Then we'll just have to finish this here," said Christine.

Mirror-Mind looked at her. "You know, the hunger is the hardest part. I can smell the life force of everyone here. I can hear every heartbeat." He stared at Christine. "I can hear it like a drumbeat, how afraid you are."

My sixth sense went off when he lunged at her, shadowy claws bared. I shot my Sticky String at him, but when it attached to his hand, he pulled me in and swatted me back with such force that I crashed through a window and into the lobby of some hotel.

I pushed myself up off the floor with shaky arms. "Come on, get up," I mumbled to myself. "You're fine. Everything's fine. It's just pain, just your body's way of telling you that you are totally not fine."

When I stumbled to my feet, I heard Christine yell, "Scar!"

She ran into the hotel through the doorway, but then, something crept out of her shadow. She sensed it, but she couldn't react in time. Mirror-Mind whacked her with the back of his hand, and she flew back, hitting her head when she hit the ground.

"Christine," I called to her.

She was unconscious ... I hoped that's all it was.

I stepped between Christine and Mirror-Mind, activating my Claws. My suit was already starting to heal me, and hopefully, Christine's would do the same for her soon. For now, I had to finish this. Mirror-Mind was too dangerous. I had to stop him.

He grinned, and the shadows around us were reacting. Dark, shadowy tentacles emerged from every darkened space in the area. They surrounded us. I stared around hopelessly, starting to think I was in over my head, but then there was a voice—deep and demonic.

"That's quite enough of that," it said.

A shadowy blade pierced through Mirror-Mind's stomach from behind, and the shadows he was controlling immediately returned to normal. He fell to the floor and bled a puddle of black.

A monstrous, six-foot-tall creature stood in his place. It had a black heart lodged halfway into its chest, and it stared at me with red, squinted eyes.

"Now, only one thing remains." When it spoke, its voice was terrifying, but it was also ... familiar.

Chapter 20

It's the alien.

The voice; the dark, muscular body; I remember it. The Adultnapper—the creatures experimenting on people, the alien at the APD's headquarters, the alien who killed my dad … and gave me my scar.

I remember.

"You're the alien," I breathed.

"And you're the human, the mistake." Its deep voice sent chills down my spine.

"What do you want with me?"

"I want you gone—eliminated. I will not have what happened in Dimention-002 repeated here."

The creature tightened its grip on its shadow sword, but my sixth sense alerted me, allowing me to act pre-emptively. I launched my Sticky String at the blade, but the creature just pulled me in with a flick of its wrist and slashed me with its claws.

I fell back to the ground, blood dripping from my face where it'd clawed me.

Then my heart began to thump rapidly; my muscles clenched and grew. I looked down at the blood dripping from my face; it was black. The scar was activating, but it wasn't two seconds ago. It's not usually this quick. I'm supposed to have more time. Did the creature do something to me?

I stood and spoke in a deep and demonic voice. "You're back."

"As are you. Though I didn't intend to see you again."

"Then perhaps you should keep away from his blood."

The creature stared at me curiously.

"You still haven't figured it out, have you? This human was born with the hybrid formula in his DNA—the child of the original hybrid. Then I was born when one of your kind touched his blood. I may not know what usually causes us to switch, but it's quite obvious that coming into contact with one of your kind will force the change."

The creature frowned. "I admit, this complicates matters. It's a good thing I came prepared."

The creature's sword disappeared into the shadows. Then, from its own shadow, a vial—filled with a purple liquid dark enough to be mistaken for black—rose to the creature's grasp. It drank the liquid and dropped the vial back into its shadow.

I just stood with my arms crossed as the creature's muscles swelled to immense size, so huge that they almost burst out of its pitch-black skin. There was a dark-purple aura surrounding its brutish body.

I laughed.

"I fail to see what's so amusing," the creature said.

"The greatest blunder of your kind is also your greatest accomplishment," I explained. "The union of human and shadow DNA is a strength unmatched. Until you learn how to produce and control the hybrids, you will always be inferior. No amount of genetic alteration will equip you to deal with me."

"Well, we're on our way to another world to continue our research anew. We will create the perfect hybrid army; we're very close. In the meantime, we shall see how capable I am of dealing with you."

The creature approached slowly. When it was just a few feet away, it stopped and looked down at me. I met its gaze, looking back up at it.

"Go ahead," I goaded.

The creature raised its club-like arm and swiftly brought it crashing down. With one hand, I stopped it and followed up with a shadow projectile, pulled from the wall and launched at its gut. Dazed, the creature stumbled backward but remained standing.

"You're stronger but not strong enough to defeat me so easily," I commented.

In response, the creature shrouded itself in a cloud of shadow, and when the cloud dispersed, the creature had multiplied into three. They ran to me, claws ready, but with another shadow projectile, I simply shot the rightmost creature, and they all fell backward.

"Doppelgangers will not fool me," I warned calmly.

The doppelgangers disappeared. The creature was drawing shadows from anywhere it could pull them to create a huge, shadowy sphere. When finished, it was the size of a bowling ball, and it was launched at me like a bullet.

I raised my hand, and with only slight difficulty, I stopped the projectile and shot it back at the creature, and this sent it backward and brought it to its knees.

It breathed heavily. "It would appear you are correct."

I raised my hands, and a shadowy mist surrounded the creature. I solidified it into jagged spikes, trained on the alien. It didn't try to fight me, and with a grin, I let the spikes penetrate its skin, and the creature died with a spray of black blood.

The alien was dead, but the nightmare wasn't over yet. The *other* me was here, and I was hungry.

The first place I turned was to Mirror-Mind's dead body, only, he wasn't there anymore. A puddle of his black blood was still there, and his clothes were still there, but he was gone. The only sign of life was the fast little heartbeat of a rat sniffing his clothes before scurrying off through the broken window I originally came through.

But there was something else, a slower heartbeat, fainter. I turned toward Christine. She was still unconscious, lying silently on the floor. This was the reason I never wanted her around me when I was the *other* me. This was my absolute worst nightmare. I looked at Christine, listened to her heart, smelled her life, and all I wanted was to eat her ... and there was no one here to stop me.

"Sarah, now!" A voice called.

"On it!" said another voice.

I was bombarded with a shadow projectile strong enough to knock me to the ground. When I returned to my feet, my attacker emerged from the shadows. She was a pale woman with short, black hair and black veins flowing throughout her body—another one of those infected people, but she seemed different somehow, less monstrous. She stared at me with cloudy, colourless eyes, and her fists were shrouded in shadows.

I grinned. "Hello, Mother."

"What did you say?" the woman responded angrily.

"Mother. You are the mother of everything that has befallen this world."

"What the hell are you on about?"

"Did you think they wouldn't put your DNA to good use?" Her heart sped up. "I am your child, and so are the hybrids loosed on the city. All this chaos was born from you."

The woman had no words, only actions. She shot me with liquefied shadows, and again I fell. She was stronger than the alien, even though she didn't look it. She fused with the darkness and reappeared in front of me, pinning me with her arm before I could get back up. I smiled at her; the *other* me didn't seem concerned. She punched me repeatedly and progressively harder, and with every punch, the shadows became more agitated, like a storm at sea. Her hand was black, and I couldn't tell if it was black with my blood or hers. I felt faint. My vision was blurry, but I could see her face, how angry she was. What did I do? What did the *other* me do?

"Sarah, stop," said another voice. "We're supposed to be subduing him, not killing him."

The woman sighed. She grabbed my face and forced my mouth open. "Hurry up."

A man crouched next to her, pulling a bottle of pink liquid from a pocket on his shirt and pouring it down my throat.

I immediately felt sleepy, but before I blacked out, I heard the man say, "What happened? Did he say something to you?"

And the woman replied. "None of your business, Sullen."

Chapter 21

My eyes slowly cracked open. The first thing I did was check my arms for black veins. There were none. I was in control again.

With that out of the way, I looked around. I was not in a hotel lobby anymore. I was lying on the floor in some sort of oval-shaped room with black walls luminous with flashing red, blue, and green lights. There was only one window that I could see, and it was curiously tinted from the inside. There also looked to be a doorway connecting this room to another one, though it was almost identical to the wall. The only way I knew it was a doorway was because it didn't have any lights.

In a corner of the room, standing in front of a wooden table was a strange-looking man mixing bottled liquids of various colours. What made the man strange-looking wasn't his clothes—though they were odd in their own right, a light-blue T-shirt filled with pockets and a bow and quiver strapped to his back—but the thing that was strange was his skin. It was completely colourless. Not colourless as in pale, colourless as in white—bone white.

The man glanced over at me and realized I was awake.

"Oh, good. You're up," he said. He walked over to me and crouched down to my level. "I was a little pressed for time when making the potion. Do you feel nauseated, have a headache or anything like that?"

"Um ... no," I said, my bewilderment almost making it sound like a question.

"Okay, that's good." He smiled and gave me a thumbs-up before returning to the table.

Then three women walked through the doorway. The door didn't even open; they just walked through as if it were made of water. The women looked just as strange as the man at the table. One of them had black dog ears coming out of her head and a fluffy dog tail from her backside. Another one looked normal enough until she opened her mouth, and I saw her huge fangs. And the last woman, I'd seen before. She was the one with black veins in her skin that beat the *other* me half to death.

"Sarah, come on," said the dog-eared woman to the black-veined one. "Just tell us what he said to you."

"It doesn't matter what he said," the black-veined woman sighed. "Just drop it."

The fanged woman chimed in. "Sarah, if we're going to work together, we have to trust each other."

The black-veined woman paused and took a breath. "I'll tell you later." Then she glanced at me. "Look who's awake."

She approached, and I flinched, hoping she wouldn't attack me again.

"Relax," she said. "I'm not going to hurt you."

My mind was full of questions, and I had no clue which one to ask first. Eventually, one just came out. "Who the hell are you people?" I probably could have worded that better, but I got my point across.

"Sarah," said the black-veined woman.

"I'm Pete," said the man with colourless skin, though he was too busy with his bottles to look up.

"Jen," said the dog-eared woman, waving at me.

The fanged woman approached and lent me her hand to help me off the floor. "I'm Vanessa."

I grabbed her hand, and she easily pulled me to my feet.

"Your hand is freezing," I commented, rubbing my hands together. "Not to sound rude," I added.

"No worries. I get that a lot." She smiled bashfully. "It's a side effect of being a vampire."

"A what?" I couldn't have heard that right.

"Vampire." Yep. That is what she said.

"You mean the ones that drink blood and turn into bats?"

"That's the one," she confirmed.

"Oh, God, where am I?" I muttered to myself. Although it was maybe a little loud to be considered a mutter.

"You are aboard my ship," said an old, wrinkly man entering through the doorway.

Vanessa moved out of his way, and the old man took her place in front of me, hobbling over using a wooden walking stick for support. His hair and moustache were grey, and he wore a white lab coat over a black shirt, and a pair of brown pants and black shoes.

"Are you all right, professor?" Vanessa asked.

"Oh, I'll be fine," he said, rubbing his back. "Just an old injury acting up."

He leaned on his walking stick with his hands draped over the top, almost like he was covering something. Maybe I was just reading too far into it. He's an old man with a back injury. Just because I'm in this strange place with these strange people, doesn't mean everything around me is suspicious.

"All right," said the old man. "Now that your scar problem has been temporarily dealt with, we can begin with a proper explanation."

"Whoa, wait, how do you know about my scar problem?"

"I know a lot about you, Alex."

"It's not as creepy as it sounds," said Sarah, leaning against the wall with her arms crossed. "The ship can look into different dimensions. We've been monitoring you."

"Yeah, sure. That sounds way less creepy." Hopefully I laid the sarcasm on thickly enough. I wasn't even going to touch the "different dimensions" thing she just said.

"I apologize for the intrusion on your privacy," the old man continued. "I assure you it was necessary to determine whether you will be a good fit."

"A good fit? For what?"

"This team, which I am assembling to combat the threat of the shadow-dwellers—the creatures who experimented on the people of your world. They are travelling to other worlds as we speak, causing similar calamities. They are a threat which I would like to thwart, and I'd like your help to do so. You are the best this world has to offer."

This was insane. He was insane, this whole place was insane, everything was insane ... But he knows what those aliens are—the aliens who killed my dad, the aliens who know the *other* me, the aliens who might even know where my mom is. How can I say no to that? Plus, despite everything that happened, I'm still an agent of the APD (kind of). It's my job to eliminate threats to society, and these aliens are a definite threat to society.

I sighed. "All right. I'll help."

"Very good." He smiled.

"What's your name, by the way? You know my name, but you never said yours."

"So I didn't. You may refer to me as Professor Thomas."

"Professor Thomas. Right. Okay, well, before we get started, I should probably go help stop the crisis we're dealing with here."

The professor waved his hand. "Oh, you needn't do that. Your comrades have already dealt with the attack on your world."

"They have? Wow. How long was I out? Or was the attack not as bad as it looked?"

The guy at the table—Pete—answered my question. "You were unconscious for about five hours."

"Five hours!" I blurted.

The dog-eared woman commented her thoughts. "I'm thinking you should have made the potion a bit weaker, Pete. You know if it were too strong, he might never have woken up."

"What!" No one seemed to notice the concern in my voice.

"I told him I was pressed for time," Pete explained. "Besides, if he were out for too long, I could have cured him ... yeah, pretty sure I could have."

"Well, on that cheery note," said the professor, "let's set a course for the next world."

"Hang on," I said. "Before we go, I've got to find Christine and let her know."

"No, I don't think that's a very good idea."

"You don't know her like I do." I started walking, in search of an exit. "Last time I left her without an explanation, things didn't go well."

"Even still, I think it would be best if you didn't tell her," he warned.

"What? No, I have to tell her. I'll only be a second."

"I said *no*!"

I stopped, and we all stared at him. I hadn't known him long, but I could tell he wasn't someone who yelled very often. Everyone was shocked.

He took a breath and walked over to me. "I apologize for having raised my voice," he said calmly, "but if you go to her now, she will die. That, I can guarantee."

"How can you possibly know that?" Sarah piped up.

"Because, Ms. Pickaro, as I've told you before, I am someone who knows."

"What's that supposed to mean?" I questioned.

"It means I've lived a very long life and seen a great many things." I stared at him blankly. "If it's of any consolation, once we've finished dealing with the threat of the shadow-dwellers, I can have you back here just moments after you leave."

"How?" I asked, suspicious.

"Time tends to be distorted between the different dimensions."

I stared at him quizzically.

"Don't believe me?" he challenged. "Take Ms. Pickaro over there." He pointed to Sarah. "At twenty-four years of age, in her world of Dimension-002, she was captured by the shadow-dwellers and studied."

"That's putting it lightly," Sarah added.

"Perhaps it is," the professor agreed. "But even still, the information they acquired was then transmitted to the shadow-dwellers here in Dimention-003, where it was used to begin what they call Project Hybrid. Their first test subject was your father, Mr. Peterson. He was given the serum as a baby and allowed to grow to maturity. He took a lovely wife, and together they had you, who possess that very same serum—Ms. Pickaro's DNA—in your genes. You have now also grown to the ripe old age of twenty-four, and here you stand before me, in the same space and time as a twenty-four-year-old Ms. Sarah Pickaro, despite these events in your lives happening over fifty years apart."

I was silent.

"I guess that makes sense." Sarah shrugged.

"There, you see?" said the professor, walking to the doorway. "Madam Time works in mysterious ways."

"Wait, what did you say?" I asked.

"It's just an expression." He didn't turn back to face me.

"No, but ... I swear I've heard that somewhere before."

"I'm sure you have, Mr. Peterson. That is the nature of an expression."

And with that, Professor Thomas retreated to the other room, and Vanessa and Jen followed him.

I walked back across the oval-shaped room, leaning on the wall next to Sarah and sighing. I didn't even have two seconds to relax before something hit me.

"Holy shit ... Sarah."

"What?" she said.

"You're the *other* me's mother, the one those aliens kept talking about."

"God, not you, too," she groaned.

"And ... the professor, he must be that traveller they kept talking about, and you're all the people he's recruiting to fight them."

"Nothing gets past you," she drawled.

I don't know why this was only now hitting me, but this felt huge. It wasn't fitting the missing piece to the puzzle of my life, but it was like finally finding where I lost that piece in the first place.

Sarah yawned, and it pulled me from my thoughts.

"Sorry," she said.

"You tired?" I wondered.

She grinned. "You have no idea." Then she looked at me quickly before resting her head back a little more comfortably on the wall. "I'm sorry, by the way, for almost beating you to death."

I looked at her. She seemed half asleep but sincere. "Don't worry about it. I'm just glad you stopped."

"Me too."

I sighed.

"Trust me, you don't want the people you love involved in any of this." Somehow, she knew exactly what I was thinking about.

"How did you—"

"It's what I'd be thinking in your situation—the people I'm leaving behind. Trust me, keep them far away from all of this. Anything else will only bring pain."

"Sounds like you're speaking from experience," I acknowledged.

She sighed. "It's a long story."

I smiled. "I've got time."

Slowly, she leaned her head forward, off the wall, and looked at me, returning the smile.

Afterword

The character of Scar is one of the oldest ideas I ever remember having. Though it's true that *Monster versus Mortal* is the first book I ever finished writing, the character of Scar is an idea I've had in my head for years before then, well before I aged into double digits. I've been writing for as long as I can remember (like, I have multiple binders full of old writing and drawings). There are a ton of ideas that I started writing but never finished, and *Scar* is the only one I've published so far that is from the pre-*Monster versus Mortal* era.

Back in those days, I used to write and draw for fun in the same way I would play video games and read books for fun, and I had school friends who would do those things with me, too, sometimes combining the mediums to make comic books together. Another person who did this with me was my cousin, and it was with him that I mostly worked on those early concepts of *Scar*. We made it into a little comic book called *The B. B. and Scar Series*, in which he handled the story of B. B. (a master of martial arts if I remember correctly), and I handled the story of

Scar (who was then an assassin with dual guns and a jetpack who got his scar-that-turns-him-into-a-monster from his criminal father, namely *The Claw*).

I've collected other pieces of writing about Scar from different points in my childhood; it was my most-written-about idea by far. When I got to the point in my life where I was capable of writing complete novels, I knew I had to properly write *Scar* at some point. So, flash forward to the age of sixteen. I'm writing the original drafts of the *Tales of the Multiverse* series, and I need a protagonist with whom to tell the story of Dimension-003. The choice was obvious. There was no better character to tell this part of the story than Alex Peterson.

At this point in my life, I was very into superhero comic books, and that greatly influenced *Scar*. (If you're into that stuff, too, you may have noticed the similarities between Scar and characters like Spider-Man, Daredevil, and the Hulk, as well as influences from various other comic book characters throughout this story.) Neetro City is a stand-in for that comic book-y American metropolis full of gritty crime and quippy humour. Many of the characters have aliases and suits that are like costumes, and the book takes itself super seriously at times and not at all seriously at others—comic books at their best (especially if you were reading a lot of stuff from the 70s like I was).

I did, however, have to assimilate *Scar* to the greater story of *Tales of the Multiverse*. That mainly came in the form of weaving the shadow-dwellers into the story. Originally, Alex's dad was a criminal named *The Claw*, as I've already said. He had a gauntlet that resembled a claw (hence the name), and he attacked his son with it. But the gauntlet had some sort of poison that reacted to Alex's DNA, and thus, the monstrous scar was born. In this new version of the story, Alex still technically gets his scar from his dad, in a manner of speaking, but his dad is no longer a criminal; he's a test subject for the shadow-dwellers, and the scar affects Alex in the way it does because his dad passed down the genes of the original hybrid to him. This also meant I had to make the *other* Alex more closely resemble Sarah and her abilities, rather than him just becoming a generic, murderous monster.

In editing the original draft of *Scar* that I wrote at sixteen to make this new version you're reading now, I noticed there was a lot in it that I'm not comfortable publishing. There were some bad depictions of mental health, abuse, and criminal activity that I feel detracted from what the book is meant to be. There's a very fine balance here between humorous and whimsical, and gritty and dark. When I was sixteen, I wrote the gritty and dark stuff a little too bluntly, and it really took away from the parts of this story that aren't supposed to be serious. When everything is said and done with this series, I wouldn't be surprised if *Scar* is the book that received the most changes out of all the *Tales of the Multiverse* books, as I had to merge characters and change entire storylines to make this book meet my current standards.

On those same lines, if you've been reading this series from *Monster versus Mortal*, you may be wondering why there is such a huge shift in tone and content rating between the books. *Monster versus Mortal* is a fantasy/mythology book that could be enjoyed by ten-year-olds. *Sarah* is a dark fantasy/romance book that's more of an ages-thirteen-and-up read. And *Scar* is more sci-fi/thriller that creeps into older teen/new adult territory. This was a choice I made right from the very beginning when I started writing this series at age twelve. I've never been the biggest fan of censorship, especially if it encroaches on the purity of a story. I didn't want to censor *Scar* just because it was in the same series as *Monster versus Mortal*, and I didn't want to make *Monster versus Mortal* any more mature than it was meant to be just to fit better with *Scar*. That would be a disservice to the books. Each book in the series is mostly its own stand-alone story. The only reason it is a series in the first place is because of the shadow-dwellers. Their story happens in the background, and as it progresses, the books in the series need to match the tone they set. In this book, the shadow-dwellers are working on Project Hybrid, which involves kidnapping and breeding people, essentially, farming human beings. So, the tone of *Scar* matches that part of their story. In *Monster versus Mortal*, the shadow-dwellers are mostly hidden, using

Monstero Academy as a front to consume the life force of monsters. Ergo, it was the sort of story that kept its more adult themes in the background, just like the shadow-dwellers. In a way, the *Tales of the Multiverse* series is one that follows the story of the shadow-dwellers from the perspectives of their enemies.

Anyway, I think that's all for this book. Next is *Planet of Shadows*, where I got to utilize my love of creature design and creating "interesting" characters. It was also the beginning of my love of languages and dialects, which I now fully utilize for the *Darphopia* series, but it started out in *Planet of Shadows*. Can't wait to see what seventeen-year-old me wrote. Until then, thanks for reading. I hope you enjoyed this book, and I hope to see you in the next one.

- R. J. F., May 2023

This is the front cover for one of *The B. B. and Scar Series* comic books that my cousin and I used to write (poor spelling included), B. B. being the one with the sword and Scar being the one with the guns. This story has come a long way from those humble beginnings.

www.ingramcontent.com/pod-product-compliance
Lightning Source LLC
Chambersburg PA
CBHW032228050726
47591CB00001B/310